A TIME TO LAUGH

Donna Winters

Bigwater Publishing LLC

www.GreatLakesRomances.com

Belen, New Mexico

A Time to Laugh Copyright © 2016 by Donna Winters

Originally released in 2005 as *Fayette—A Time to Laugh*

Great Lakes Romances® is a registered trade-mark of

Bigwater Publishing LLC
334 Sunrise Blf
Belen, NM 87002

ISBN-13: 978-0-923048-96-9
ISBN-10: 0-923048-96-0

Edited by Pamela Quint Chambers and Nancy Kane
Front cover image of woman © Kathy Dewar

To all who love Fayette Historic Townsite

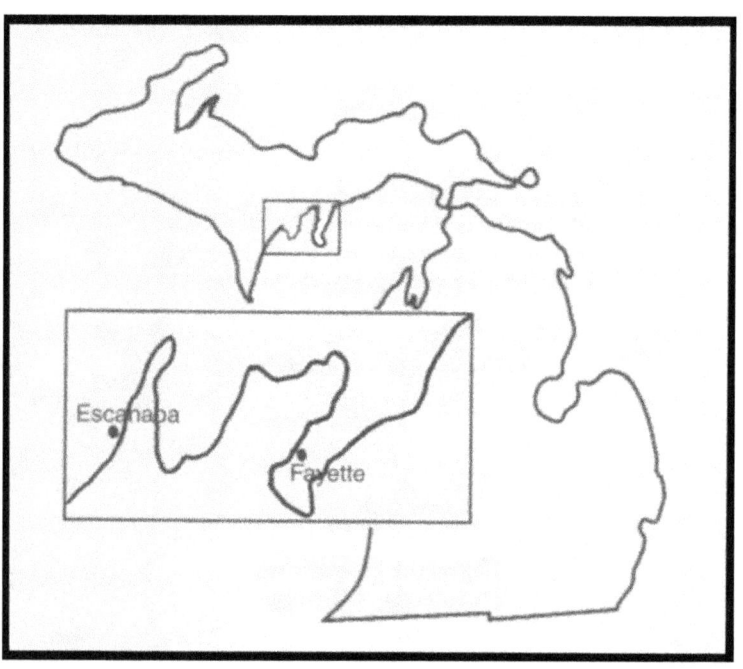

CONTENTS

CHAPTER 1

Fayette, Michigan
Wednesday, September 3, 1879

Preoccupied with her intention to fill her baskets with fresh vegetables at the village garden on Furnace Hill, eighteen-year-old Flora McAdams didn't miss her copper-colored dog, Stubby, until she heard an angry shout from the Machine Shop she had just passed.

"Get out, you miserable mutt!"

Flora whirled around. A scowling machinist snapped an oily rag at Stubby's nose.

He yelped and scurried back to her, tail down.

Flora glared at the machinist. "Good glory! Can't you see he's an old dog that wouldn't hurt a flea?"

The fellow crossed his arms on his homespun vest. His chiseled countenance was stone cold, his blue-gray eyes casting a clear message of condemnation. Without a word, he disappeared inside the brick building, his wavy light-brown hair tousled by the lake breeze that chased after his svelte, nearly six-foot-tall frame.

Flora set down her baskets to comfort Stubby, then told him to sit and stay. Pushing back her hat, the straw one with the notch in the brim that a cat had bitten off, she strode into the noisy shop. Ignoring Louis Follo, the machinist she'd known for quite some time, she headed straight for the dog-loathing fellow. Coming to a halt one foot from his face, she stood as erect as her five-foot-four-inch height would allow and shook her finger at him.

"Don't you ever hit my dog again! Is that clear?"

He grasped her firmly by the elbow and escorted her out the door despite her foot-dragging.

"No dogs allowed. Women, either. Too dangerous." His Scandinavian-accented words were calm but indisputable. With a dip of his head, he turned to go.

Flora watched his determined stride carry his lean, solid form and straight back into the shop once more. She followed on his heels and tapped him on the shoulder, letting loose with a torrent of words the moment he faced her.

"You ought to be kinder to animals, especially dogs. One of them will turn on you and tear you apart one of these days if you keep snapping at them the way you did. Then you'll be sorry!"

His rugged countenance darkened. "Dogs are nuisance, distraction. Like you. Now, go!"

He reached for her but she backed all the way to the door. "You'll be sorry, mark my words!" She spun away and exiting, her head held high.

Outside the shop again, she picked up her baskets, her mind racing. Why had she never seen this fellow before?

She knew practically everyone after eleven years at the pig iron village.

But Mr. Schiling, the former machinist whose hand had been crushed in a Machine Shop accident had spoken of his replacement. A single man was coming to town who would board at Mrs. Lindberg's. This fellow with the snapping oily rag evidently was that new man.

Pushing the troubling encounter from her mind, Flora set off again for the garden. As she passed the railroad grade, the granary, and the jail that had been newly built this year, she made certain that Stubby remained close by her side despite the loose dogs that tempted to lure him away on ventures of his own.

Too many stray dogs and cats roamed in the village, getting hurt or injured. She needed to harvest whatever was ripe in the garden and sell it at Harris's market, as she had been doing for a while now, so she could replenish her diminishing supplies of rubbing alcohol, witch hazel, cotton batting, and the tinctures she used to nurse wounded or sick creatures to health.

It had all started when she was only seven, and her older brother, Toby, had found a family of orphaned baby foxes. Ever since, she'd been on a mission to care for helpless creatures. For a time, she had offered care to small wild animals as well as fellow townspeople's family pets. Then, after a couple of bouts of mange passed to her and Stubby from wild things, and stern lectures from the company doctor on the possibility of contracting rabies, she had restricted her services to the community's pets. Just yesterday she had treated a neighbor's small, white dog that had an open sore, and had taken in a yellow cat with a hairball problem. The cat was still under observation in a cage in the back yard.

Of course, her animal welfare wouldn't have been possible without the patience and tutoring of Dr. Bellows, the company doctor, who had taught her over the years how to apply his people-healing knowledge to lesser creatures in need. Dr. Bellows, with his neatly trimmed salt and pepper beard and mustache, had been like a kind uncle, never too busy for her questions and always interested in her newest patient. Just as he had established his reputation as the healer for the people of Fayette, she had developed her own reputation as the healer for the animals. For a long time now, anyone who owned a hurt dog or cat was told, "Take it to Flora McAdams. She'll know what to do." She frequently thanked God for the good doctor's tutoring and kindness.

Her thoughts turning again to the vegetable garden, she thanked God, too, for the fair weather He had provided today. Trekking up Hill Street behind the iron furnace, she prayed for a good harvest on this fine day. Pausing at her destination, she turned toward the soft wind, strands of hair fluttering against her face beneath the broad brim of her straw hat as she took in the sky and sea. Wisps of gossamer floated on faded cerulean silk in the heavens above, and crystal chips crested quiet waves on the water of the bay below. The sun shone warm upon her shoulders, tempering the coolness of the lake breeze and turning this day into a gardener's dream.

She gazed down at the town a-bustle with the business of pig iron production. Fayette had grown in the eleven years she had been living here. The furnace had doubled in size, with a second stack and casting house standing beside the original structures to improve pig iron production. And in support of the business expansion, new homes and businesses had sprung up.

Log cabins jammed the alley near the shoreline. Frame homes lined Stewart and Sheldon Avenues, and more were being built here on Hill Street and down on Portage Avenue. The hotel had gained a second story, and the Town Hall had been built across from it. The Carpenter's Shop had replaced a shed years ago, and now the shop was being rebuilt.

Warehouses, the Company Office, stock barns, and charcoal kilns had risen over the years or been rebuilt. But the most important addition to Fayette according to Mama and Papa had been the schoolhouse constructed farther up the hill. Away from the commotion of the furnace activity and construction sites, it served not only to improve the minds of the sixty or so regular scholars, but as a place of worship as well. And now its bell was ringing loud and clear, bidding students in grades one through eight to enter in for another day of learning.

The tapping of carpenters' hammers played counterpoint to the school bell and the distant clanging of the iron moulders' sledge hammers in the casting houses below. Compounding the rhythm was the chugging of the furnace train headed down the track to collect another load of charcoal.

One thing hadn't much changed over the years, though. The air still carried the odor of furnace smoke, more noticeable when both stacks were in blast as they were now. But today the blessed breeze carried the smoke away from Flora, out across the water.

Another thing that hadn't changed was the beauty of the harbor. A small spit of land still curved gently into the shape of a snail shell for which the port was named, and the tall limestone bluff, despite the ravages of commercial endeavor, still rose majestically along its eastern shore. Yes, some of the limestone nearest the furnace had clearly been chipped away, mined off to serve as flux for the furnaces and for mortar, chinking, and plaster for Fayette and nearby Escanaba, but the grand nature of the bluff remained impressive as ever.

Greetings to her from a latecomer on his route to school interrupted Flora's reminiscences and brought her back to her intended task at the garden. With a command to Stubby to lie down and stay at the edge of the patch, she stepped carefully among the tomato plants in search of ripe fruit.

Finding little, she left her family's plot to inspect the Schiling patch that had been left to her care and harvesting when Mr. Schiling had lost the use of his hand in the Machine Shop accident and moved away. To her delight, several tomatoes had ripened overnight, and his cucumbers, beans, and melons appeared ready for picking also. She set to work, humming an Irish ditty that her older sister's husband, Huck, had taught her years ago.

The song took her back in time again to her first year at Fayette when Lavinia and Huck had fallen in love and decided to get married. Even at age seven Flora remembered how unmistakably right the match had been; though her sister had tried for a time to deny it. At age seventeen Lavinia had wed. It was the same age at which Mama had married Papa, but Flora broke that tradition.

Among her acquaintances of the masculine gender, not a one was now, nor had ever been closer than a friend. There was Henry Pinchin, her neighbor across the way who clerked at the company store, and Joseph Marew at the butcher shop, always ready with a bone for Stubby. She counted Thomas Young, the owner of the cat she was caring for, among her friends; John Meehan, too, new to the town last year and known for his phenomenal memory. Nevertheless, her seventeenth year had come and gone, and without regrets, none of these fellows had become suitors.

Perhaps her concern and devotion to animals in need had simply overridden the notions of love and romance and the hints of such from fellow friends—at least that's what Grandma had told her. But Flora disagreed. She was acutely aware that, by comparison to her sister and mother and some of the other young ladies in the town, she was endowed with a decidedly plain face and sturdy frame. But that mattered not at all to the animals she helped heal and their human keepers who appreciated her skill. Because of them she felt no lack of love and affection in her life.

She moved to the next row of beans. A few more would fill the second of her two baskets. She stooped to continue her harvesting and her humming, calculating how much her fresh produce would bring at Harris's market. A tidy sum was dominating her thoughts when a shadow crept over the bean bush she was picking.

The shadow had not been cast by a cloud, she was certain, for it formed the distinctive shape of a human figure—a male figure. She left off her humming and glanced up through the notch in the brim of her straw hat. To her dismay, the shadow belonged to none other than the machinist with whom she'd had her earlier encounter. Only now, he wore a broad-brimmed brown plush hat.

He gazed down at her with mild displeasure. "I'll be hanged! You again!"

"Good glory, I thought I'd left you back at the Machine Shop." She rose to her feet to toss the last of her harvest into her basket and look for Stubby. But he was nowhere in sight. She assumed the machinist would begin to complain about her dog, but instead, his tone was congenial in the extreme.

"Please, can you tell? Where is Schiling garden?"

At his question, Flora noticed the basket he held. *"This* is the Schiling garden, but you'll find no ripe vegetables to pick. Mr. Schiling told me I could tend his garden and harvest it. No need for his fruits and vegetables to go to weed and waste, he said. I don't suppose he thought you'd have need of a garden. He said you were a single man, that you'd be a boarder at Mrs. Lindberg's." She named the boarding house next door to her own home on Stewart Avenue.

He nodded. "I come to get vegetables for Mrs. Lindberg, get credit on my bill. Ja?" His gaze shifted to the two full baskets beside Flora.

"I take my harvest to Harris' market. The money I make goes for medical supplies for the sick animals I tend. Those dogs you so dislike get into fights, and encounters with porcupines, and every manner of mischief. There must be a hundred of them in the village and I have no lack of patients in need of care, besides the cats folks bring me." Reaching for one of her filled baskets, she continued. "But I would never want to come between you and your boarding bill. Here, take this to Mrs. Lindberg. She should be willing to give you a handsome credit for such fine produce as this." She offered him the basket brimful of melons and string beans.

"I cannot," the fellow said, putting up his hand.

The lunch hour whistle sounded. Flora placed the basket over her arm and picked up her other basket. "Then *I'll* take it to Mrs. Lindberg and tell her to credit your account. Good day Mr. . . . ?"

"Jorgensen. Sven Jorgensen. And you are?"

"Late for lunch. Good day, Mr. Jorgensen."

CHAPTER 2

Flora headed down Hill Street hoping she wasn't too late to meet up with Papa and Toby who would be coming out of the furnace casting house. She could use their help carrying her baskets home. She searched for Papa's bare, balding head and Toby's blue tweed cap in the stream of men disbursing for their midday meal. Giving up hope of finding them, she had continued on her way when they came up on either side of her and lifted the baskets off her arms.

"Are these for lunch?" Papa's blue eyes twinkled as he held up a plump tomato. Not waiting for a reply, he took a bite. Juice ran down his clean-shaven chin and rugged hand. "Mm. This is an exceptionally fine tomato. Our garden is better than ever this year, don't you think?"

Flora laughed. "I hate to spoil your illusion, Papa, but that tomato came from Mr. Schiling's garden."

"And here I thought you were becoming a master gardener."

"I wish that were so." She grew silent, aware that Sven was close behind. When they neared Lindbergs', she took the basket of melons and green beans from Toby. "I'll be right home. I need to drop this off for Mrs. Lindberg."

"Wasn't that basket for Harris's?" Toby's brow rose.

Flora shook her head. "I'll explain later." With Sven at her heels, she marched to the back of the Lindberg place. The aroma of fried beef and onions wafted through the kitchen's screen door. The clamor of pans and the voices of her friend, Elin, and her mother, indicated their hurry to serve the twelve boarders.

Flora let herself in, greeted by Elin. To Flora's dismay, Sven followed her through the door. She ignored him and returned the greeting of her tall, blonde friend, then addressed her equally tall and blonde mother who was busy at the stove.

"These melons and beans are to be credited to Mr. Jorgensen's account." She explained how she had encountered Mr. Jorgensen while she had been harvesting the Schiling garden and that the boarder assumed he was entitled to them and wished a credit with Mrs. Lindberg in exchange.

Sven, who had remained politely silent while Flora spoke, now stepped forward as if to protest, but before he could speak, Mrs. Lindberg came at him, shaking her wooden spoon and addressing him sharply. "Boarders not allowed in kitchen! Go!"

Instantly he headed out the door.

Elin took Flora's basket. "Look at the beautiful melons, Mama."

"Bless you, Flora. Mr. Jorgensen will get credit."

"Thanks, Mrs. Lindberg. Good day."

"See you tonight, Flora?" Elin asked.

"After supper." Flora looked forward to the time they often spent together after Elin had helped her mother wash supper dishes and set places for breakfast at the boarding house.

At the pump behind her own home next door, Flora scrubbed the garden dirt from her hands and beneath her nails. At the back of the yard, Stubby lay asleep beneath his favorite shade tree. She silently thanked God for the eleven years she'd had with her favorite four-footed companion.

Not far away, the cat with the hairball was lying comfortably in his cage. After lunch she would bring him some leftovers. Now, she had to get inside.

Papa had set the basket he'd carried for her just inside the back door, out of Stubby's reach, and safe from any other four-footed or winged creatures that might be tempted to sample her harvest. After lunch, she would wash some tomatoes and cucumbers for Mama and Grandma and take what was not needed for her own family's supper to Harris's market. It wouldn't bring much, but enough to keep her in supplies until more melons and beans ripened.

She took her place at the table across from her small-in-stature but quite opinionated grandmother who had been living with her family for eleven years. Beside her sat her older brother, Toby, who was now a strapping young fellow of twenty-three with a job of his own at the furnace casting house. Papa asked a blessing, then

helped himself to a biscuit and the liver stew and passed
them on. When all had filled their plates, and a blessing
was said, Mama, whose dark, center-parted hair seemed
to gain more silver streaks with each passing year,
opened conversation. Her gaze was squarely on Papa,
who sat opposite her at the other end of the table.

"When I went to the Company Store this morning for
some thread to do the mending, I heard the most exciting
news in many a month in this town."

Papa paused in his pursuit of the stew long enough to
cock his brow and inquire, "What's that, dear?"

Mama smiled broadly, the glow of her countenance in
sharp contrast to the drab gray of her dress. "A ball is to
be held in the Town Hall on the third of October. That's
only one month away!"

"Is that so?" Papa replied casually between bites.
"Didn't we just have a masquerade ball a couple of
months ago?"

Mama shook her head. "That was back in February.
Don't you remember that Lavinia and Huck came up
from Sac Bay to stay overnight, and we took them to the
ball while Flora and Toby watched the three children?"

Papa reached for another biscuit. "Ah, yes. I remember. The youngest was so little she kept waking me up
with her crying in the middle of the night."

"Well, she's past that now." Mama's tone sweetened.
"You *will* take me to the ball, won't you, Angus?"

He smiled. "Of course, dear, and Lavinia and Huck,
too, if they want to go."

"Toby and I can watch the children again." Flora
tucked into her stew.

Grandma's stooped shoulders straightened, the knot of silver hair atop her head adding height to her diminutive form. "Not this time. *I'll* watch the children. You and Toby go to the ball with your friends and enjoy yourselves."

"But I don't *want* to go to the ball," Flora insisted. "Whose idea was it to hold a ball, anyway?"

"Alison Kitchen and Harriet Harris thought of it." Mama named the wife of the company superintendent, J.B. Kitchen, and the wife of the former superintendent, Joseph Harris, the man who now ran the town's only hotel. "They claim it will be the most beautiful event ever held in iron country."

Papa paused in buttering his biscuit. "Those ladies do tend to set the standard for style where social events are concerned."

Mama nodded. "If not for them, we'd be reduced to baseball games and horse races to socialize with one another in the evenings. And you know how I feel about all the wagering that takes place on horses and baseball scores."

"I'm not sure the ball will eliminate the problem. Someone's sure to institute a raffle with the drawing to be held at the ball." Papa bit into his biscuit.

Mama sighed. "I suppose you're right. I hadn't thought of that."

"But if the raffle raises money for a good cause, then it's not so bad, is it?" Flora's gaze met Mama's. "I'd like to institute a raffle of my own and raise money for animal welfare."

"What would *you* raffle off? One of those stray dogs you're always fixing up?" Toby snickered.

"Certainly *not!* You don't find a good owner for a dog by picking someone at random." Flora's tone softened. "Besides, nobody would buy a raffle ticket for a dog in a town where there are strays a-plenty and more puppies being born all the time that need homes. I wonder, though. Who has something really wonderful that they'd be willing to donate to my cause?"

"Raffle or no, I think a ball is just what this town needs this fall." Grandma dabbed at the corners of her mouth with her napkin. "Why, when I was a young lass back in Scotland, we seldom had such activities to attend. A ball is just the thing to help civilize some of the young bachelors in this town. They need a reason to put on their finest suits, *and manners*, and socialize with marriageable young ladies under proper conditions."

Flora stabbed a piece of liver. "Well I, for one, will *not* be among the young ladies they meet. I have all the friends I need. Besides, I have no dress to wear, no grace for dance steps, and neither the time, the money, nor the inclination to make up for my shortcomings." She popped the liver into her mouth.

Grandma shook a crooked finger. "Now see here, Flora—"

"Mother," Mama's tone brooked no argument. "Flora is old enough to decide for herself whether she will or will not attend. Although I'm willing to presume that you would make over an old dress of mine or Lavinia's to suit the occasion, should Flora change her mind."

Grandma beamed. "I'd be most happy to."

Papa grinned. "And I'd be happy to help Flora with her dancing."

Mama turned to Flora. "So you see, dear? There's no need to miss out on what is sure to be the most delightful event ever planned for Fayette."

"But, Mama—"

"One more thing, Flora," Mama's tone was confidential. "Harriet has told me that Big Toby is already in quite a dither over the ball." She referred to an employee at the hotel, a longtime family friend who was like an older brother to Flora—a tall fellow with striking good looks who was several years her senior—but he was not quite right in the head.

Mama continued. "Harriet says Big Toby wants more than anything to attend the ball, but he's scared to death no one will go with him, and afraid that if he showed up alone, no one would dance with him. If Big Toby should ask you, Flora, would you at least give it some consideration? It might be his only opportunity to experience such a lovely night out."

Flora had always held a soft spot in her heart for Big Toby, whose only living relative, an aunt, had passed away a few months ago. She would no more think of turning him down than of turning away an injured dog or cat in need of her care. "Of course I'll go with him if he asks, Mama."

"God bless you, sweetheart."

"Now who can we get to go with your brother?" Grandma's brow furrowed.

Toby chuckled. "I don't know anyone who would want to go with me."

Grandma turned to Mama. "Mrs. Harris didn't mention any young ladies in need of an escort, did she?"

"Grandma!" Toby objected.

Grandma shrugged. "Just thought I'd ask."

"Surely there's a young lady somewhere in this town who's just waiting for you to ask her, son." Papa smiled. "What about Elin, next door?"

The unmistakable ruckus of a dogfight nearby eliminated any answer Toby might have offered. At the snarls, growls, yelps, and the frantic barking of Stubby, Flora sprang from her seat.

CHAPTER 3

Flora grabbed a broom on her way through the kitchen and Grandma's quarters at the back of the house. A black pup with white feet was in a scuffle with a brown pup over a basket of spilt produce. Nearby, old Stubby barked and growled in a failed effort to warn them off.

Flora charged toward them, broom swinging. "Shoo! Go on! Git!" A few harmless swats to the backsides of both animals sent them scurrying away, tails between their legs. Stubby trotted immediately to her side, sniffing out the scents left by the intruders and sampling what was left behind.

"Stubby, leave it!" Flora commanded.

He backed away and lay down with a sigh.

Flora silently thanked God that at least in his old age Stubby had learned not to enter into the fray with two younger, feistier pups. She and Dr. Bellows had sewn him up a few times following the indiscretions of his youth and she didn't relish the procedure.

She turned her attention to the mess, muttering to herself. "Good glory. Green beans scattered everywhere, and smashed melons besides."

The rest of the family came out back to help while the yellow cat with the hairball meowed loudly from his cage.

Toby stooped to survey two damaged melons. "Aren't these the melons I carried for you?"

"I'm afraid so." Flora recognized her basket and turned to Papa. "When I left the melons and beans with Mrs. Lindberg and Elin, they were very pleased to have them. How do you suppose they ended up here, the object of a dog fight?"

"Evidently *someone* at Mrs. Lindberg's wasn't pleased with your pickings." He rested his hand on Toby's shoulder. "We've got work to do. See you at suppertime."

Flora gave a nod and then stooped to clean up the mess with the help of Mama and Grandma.

"What a waste of fine melon," Grandma lamented. "But the beans still look good. I'll get a basin. We can wash them and cook them for supper."

Mama reached for a chunk of cantaloupe and held it to her nose. "Mm. Just at the peak of ripeness, too."

When they had finished putting the scraps into the basket, Mama said, "This afternoon, we'd better can the tomatoes and pickle the cucumbers you picked this morning. I'm counting on your help after the dishes are done."

"I'll be in as soon as I feed some of this to Stubby and give the cat some butter."

While Flora fed the dog and gave butter to the cat to help move the hairball through his system, she pondered Papa's words, coming to the only conclusion that could explain the returned basket. Sven Jorgensen had protested her leaving the basket of beans and melons with Mrs. Lindberg, and he was the one who had set them on the back stoop.

Despite Flora's promise to Mama, she headed for the Machine Shop, the basket of waste on her arm and words of reprimand on her mind. From the open door at the back of the shop she could see Louis Follo working at the metal lathe while Sven looked on. She shouted Sven's name above the noise.

When he saw her, he came outside to stand before her, arms crossed on his vest, a look of pure chagrin on his face.

"Look at this!" Flora held up the basket of melon scraps. "Wasted! Destroyed by stray dogs. And all because of you! What were you thinking, leaving a basket of food outside unattended? You should have knocked and given it to me in person if you were so set against letting Mrs. Lindberg keep it. You're stubborn as a mule, do you know that, Mr. Jorgensen?"

"*I'm* stubborn?" He uncrossed his arms and pointed his finger in her face. "*You're* more stubborn than a whole *train* of mules!"

Flora remained momentarily silent, unable to prevent the smile that crept over her face, or the laughter that welled up inside and spilled out. Soon, Sven was laughing too.

When the joyful sound had died away, the two of them simply stood gazing at one another. The gray in Sven's eyes had turned a friendly shade of blue, and a smile softened his mouth. Flora tried to think of something to say, but suddenly she was tongue-tied. She should turn and go, but her feet seemed mired in clay.

When he broke the silence between them, his quiet words rang sincere. "I am sorry. I never leave food outside again."

"I forgive you."

Flora somehow managed to wrench her gaze from his tall, slender frame and head for home. Butterflies fluttered in her stomach, and though her feet crunched against the slag-covered roadway, they seemed not quite under her. She couldn't get the mellow tone of Sven's voice or his words out of her head.

But when she arrived at her back yard, the meowing of the cat and the gentle nudge of Stubby reminded her of the problem still at hand. On her arm hung a basketful of wasted produce, none of it destined for Harris's market to earn money for the animal welfare supplies she so desperately needed. When she had fed more of the melon to Stubby, she set the leftovers just inside the back door and headed for the kitchen.

Mama greeted her. "Where have you been, Flora? Grandma and I were counting on your help."

Grandma's disapproving gaze chased thoughts of Sven from Flora's mind. "At least you're here now. Get yourself a knife and a cutting board and dice the tomatoes fine for cold catsup."

"Cold catsup?"

"I found this recipe in the paper last week." Grandma tapped an arthritic finger on a clipping that lay on the table.

Flora quickly read the recipe. "Grandma, do you think I could sell this catsup at Harris's market?"

"Why on earth would you want to do that?"

"Because I need the money for supplies. I hardly have anything left for taking care of the animals. And you know how quickly the dogs in this village get into trouble and end up here to be patched up."

"Can't you borrow what you need from Dr. Bellows? After all, he must have a budget for such things from the company. I should think he'd be willing to give you what you need, seeing as how the dogs and cats you treat belong to company employees or are the offspring of their pets."

Flora sighed. "Dr. Bellows has already given me plenty, and spent lots of time teaching me how to fix up injured creatures. I just can't impose on him for more handouts."

Grandma scowled. "Far too much of your time and effort is wasted on those animals, and not nearly enough of it learning from your mother and me how to cook and sew and keep house. Most young ladies your age are employed in domestic work, after all, out cooking and cleaning and caring for small children. They're gaining worthwhile experience that will stand them in good stead when they become wives and mothers themselves. Take Mary Caffey, for example, or her sister Johanna. Then there's Ella Rabarge helping to care for Sam Kitchen's brood of four."

Flora's heart sank. She'd heard Grandma's opinion on her animal welfare efforts in the past. She would never earn approval for them. But the thought of working as a domestic held no appeal.

Mama reached across the table and patted her hand. "Surely there must be a way to earn some money, but I don't think you should try and sell this cold catsup at Harris's. After all, this is our first time making it. We'd better try it ourselves before you put any of it up for sale." She thought a moment. "There is something you *can* make that's a sure thing for cash. You can make it up right here, right now, and have it ready to peddle outside the furnace when the men get out of work at five o'clock."

Grandma sent a puzzled look in Mama's direction.

Flora waited with great expectation.

Mama smiled. "Why don't you bake a couple of batches of taffy tarts?"

"Taffy tarts! What a wonderful idea!" Flora's mouth began to water at the thought of Papa's favorite dessert.

Grandma nodded. "I can't imagine anyone not liking taffy tarts."

"But . . ." Flora grew thoughtful. "Grandma, I don't know *how* to bake taffy tarts."

"It's high time you learned. I may not be real fond of your reason for baking them, but if it will get you interested in learning how to do more in the kitchen than just boiling water for tea, then I'm all for it. Get yourself a couple of mixing bowls and your mother and I will tell you what to do."

Flora followed directions exactly, mixing together flour, salt, lard, and a little water for the crust, rolling it out and cutting it to size, and lining the tart pans. Then, she beat two eggs and measured out the brown sugar, vanilla, salt, and butter precisely as she was told for the filling. When the first batch of taffy tarts had been put into the oven to bake, Mama headed over to the school to deliver an invitation to the two new schoolteachers to come for tea after school on Friday. By the time she returned, the first batch of tarts had come out of the oven and the second batch had been put in to bake.

Mama deeply inhaled the enticing aroma, and inspected the tarts that were cooling on the table.

"Mm, mm. I don't see how anyone could pass these by without purchasing at least one. They look and smell absolutely wonderful and I'm sure they'll taste delicious. Fine job, Flora." She offered a beaming smile and a hug.

"Thank you, Mama."

She nodded, her smile fading as her gaze lingered on Flora. "Now, about Friday. Mr. Mason and Miss Ruggles have both accepted my invitation to tea and I expect you to be here and to help Grandma and me to make these two fine young people welcome. You could bake up a fresh batch of taffy tarts just before they come. You know how much it means to me to encourage our teachers and to have good schooling offered to all who wish to learn."

"Yes, Mama." Flora silently reminisced about the very first classes at Fayette, taught by Mama at their dining room table eleven years ago. Even though Flora dreaded such social encounters as Mama had planned for the teachers, she resigned herself to the annual ritual established when the schoolhouse had been built and the first teacher hired. Pushing thoughts of the upcoming event from her mind, she focused on washing and wiping and putting away the bowls, cups, and spoons that had been used for tart dough and filling. By half-past four, the second batch of tarts came out of the oven, golden brown and smelling too delicious to resist.

When they had cooled a little, Mama helped her set them on a doily lined tray along with a jar for collecting the money, and she offered some advice.

"Remember, Flora, that when the whistle blows and the men come out of the furnace, they're going to have one thing on their minds and one thing only—getting home to supper. You're going to have to make yourself heard loud and clear if you're to sell your wares."

Grandma nodded. "Call out like this: 'Taffy tarts, fresh from the oven, a penny apiece! Get your taffy tart! Tasty and sweet!' Then start all over again."

Mama smiled. "And don't be afraid to ask for donations in addition to the penny for the tart. After all, you've patched up lots of family pets at absolutely no cost to their owners. It wouldn't hurt some of those fellows to give a little extra in return."

"Yes, Mama." Flora didn't want to ask for handouts when some of the laborers made barely enough to support their families, but she supposed Mama's idea had merit where the skilled workers were concerned.

She donned her straw hat, picked up her tray, and headed for the door. Then she paused and turned back. "Mama, Grandma, thanks for all your help. Say a little prayer for me, that I'll be home soon with a jar full of pennies."

"We will," Mama promised.

"You'll do fine," Grandma said confidently. "I've never known a man who didn't like taffy tarts."

With those words ringing in Flora's ears, she headed out the door and hurried toward the furnace. Halfway there, she whispered a prayer of her own that she would not be completely overlooked in the mad rush for home at the changing of the twelve-hour shift, and that her tarts would sell quickly.

CHAPTER 4

It seemed that Flora's prayer for brisk tart sales was being answered when a half-dozen men waiting to start the night shift at the casting house each purchased a tart and began telling others to do the same. By the time the whistle blew, a third of her inventory had been depleted.

In a rush, the laborers surged from the casting houses, voices loud as they celebrated the end of their toil for the day and greeted the night shift replacements. Flora had to shout to be heard above the din. At first, it seemed as if the sea of humanity would swallow her up and drown her out.

Then Thomas Young and John Meehan came along. Thomas gave her a penny for the tart and an additional three pennies for tending his cat. John took one bite of his tart and quickly bought two more. Then Papa and Toby came out.

With them doing the hawking, she not only sold the remaining tarts quickly, but also gained several donations as Papa shamed owners of Flora's former patients into giving extra.

Just as the last tart disappeared from Flora's tray and into the mouth of a laborer, she caught sight of Sven, a penny in his hand.

"Too late?" he asked.

Flora looked up through the notch in the brim of her hat and replied with a rueful smile. "Sorry, Mr. Jorgensen. The tarts are all gone."

He dropped his penny in her jar. "Next time, you owe me."

"But—"

"You owe me!" He wagged his finger.

Flora opened her mouth to argue, but he disappeared in the crowd.

Papa took the collection jar from her tray and shook it. "I'd guess there's about half a day's pay worth of coins in there." He handed the jar back to Flora.

Toby smiled ruefully. "And it didn't take nearly that long to collect, either."

Flora returned his smile. "But it did take me most of the afternoon to bake the tarts."

Toby's eyes rolled skyward. "You get no sympathy from me. Kitchen work isn't nearly so hot and heavy as molding iron pigs."

Flora laughed. "Thank goodness for that."

Toby took her empty tray and carried it under his arm. When Papa had gone a few steps ahead, talking to one of the men that he supervised at the furnace, Toby quietly asked Flora, "Is Elin coming over tonight?"

"Yes, why?" Then Flora remembered the question that had come up at the midday meal. "Are you thinking of asking her to go to the ball with you?"

He shrugged. "Do you think she would?"

"Ask her and find out, silly!"

A doubtful look settled on his countenance. "Do you think you could sort of . . ."

"Ask her in advance how she would feel about the possibility of you inviting her to the ball?"

Toby nodded.

"I'll see what I can find out."

After a moment's silence, Toby said, "Did you hear? Dr. Bellows' horse is going up against T. J. Streeter's tonight at the track."

"Good glory! That will be a great race! I hope Dr. Bellows wins. We can't let that out-of-town stallion from Sac Bay take the honors."

Toby gave her a nudge. "Maybe you and Elin could go over to the track with me." His invitation was a clear departure from his normal habit of attending the races with fellows from work.

"Maybe," Flora replied nonchalantly. Then she laughed. "Of course we'll go with you—at least I'm pretty sure Elin will want to. I, for one, wouldn't dream of missing this race."

Even though Mama and Grandma disapproved of the races because of the betting, Flora felt a personal responsibility to show support for her dear friend and mentor whenever his horse went out on the track. And Papa and Toby felt the same, enjoying the excitement of the contests without the need to gamble. Most often, the competition was completely local among the horses of Dr. Bellows, the hotel manager Joe Harris, and the Superintendent J.B. Kitchen. Flora looked forward with special interest to the contest tonight because of the out-of-town horse coming in.

But first, she looked forward to counting the coins in the jar she was carrying. The moment she walked in the door, she went straight to the kitchen.

"Mama, Grandma, look!" She held up the jar.

Mama pushed aside the bowl and spoons on the kitchen table. "Dump your money out and count it."

Moments later, with the help of Mama and Grandma, she had totaled her earnings.

"Eighty cents! Can you believe it?" Flora scooped the pennies up, dropped them into the jar, and set it in the cupboard beside the old sugar bowl that held the family emergency money. "Tomorrow, I'll visit Mr. Powell and buy supplies." She referred to the new Company Store manager. "I wonder if he'll be willing to give me a little extra for my money the way Mr. Pinchin did. He always threw in a nickel's worth more to help me with the animals."

Mama shrugged. "I wouldn't plan on any extra if I were you. When I was in the store today I couldn't help noticing that prices are higher since Mr. Powell took over, and he didn't budge one inch when Mrs. Harris tried to tease him into giving her a little extra ribbon for her granddaughter's hair." She wiped the table. "Now go wash up. Grandma and I are ready to serve supper."

At the supper table, Toby was even quieter than usual. Flora wondered if he was thinking over what he might say to Elin.

When the meal ended, Flora fed Stubby and the cat leftover chowder along with more of the smashed melons and beans, then helped Mama and Grandma clean up and wash dishes. As soon as the last clean dish had been wiped and put away, she headed next door to tell Elin about the horse race and help her finish her chores in time to get to the track.

Flora wasn't at all surprised that Toby had expressed an interest in her willowy friend whose fair countenance often wore the blush of English roses and a smile that quickly turned to lighthearted laughter. The halo of blond braid crowning her head, the aspect of pure innocence about her, and an attitude of kindness suggested an angel in human form, and Flora sometimes had to repent the sin of envy over her friend's beauty, both inner and outer. But Elin, being of Swedish stock, kept her feelings close to her heart and Flora had no idea what she thought of Toby where social possibilities were concerned. Perhaps she could find out by using the invitation to tonight's race as a barometer.

Flora was no sooner inside the Lindberg kitchen door than Elin said, "You were all the talk at dinner tonight. Some fellows bought your tarts." She clicked her tongue and moved her head from side to side, a teasing smile in place.

"What did they say?" Flora demanded.

Elin turned to her mother. "Should I tell, Mama?"

"Speak the truth," Mrs. Lindberg said somewhat sternly.

Elin laughed. "The men think you should sell tarts every day!"

Mrs. Lindberg smiled. "Especially Mr. Jorgensen."

Flora chuckled. "I do owe him a tart. But I don't plan to bake them every day."

Flora turned the conversation to the news of the race that would be held at the track tonight, and the ball that was being planned for the third of October. When Mrs. Lindberg carried the food scraps outside, Flora told Elin, "Toby invited us to go with him over to the race track tonight. I told him I thought you would want to go. Do you?"

She watched Elin carefully, finding a definite sparkle in her blue eyes despite her placid tone when she said simply, "I would like that."

"Good. Let's finish up here so we can get to the track in time."

They put away the clean dishes and set the table for breakfast, then Elin went to freshen up and Flora went home to do the same. She found Toby in his room upstairs, carefully combing his hair and tucking in his shirt while studying himself in his mirror.

"I'm sure Elin will think you look just fine." Flora described her friend's sparkling eyes when told of Toby's invitation to the race. "Once you and Elin get to talking, I'll conveniently disappear."

"All right, but don't go far. What do I do if I run out of things to say?"

Flora grinned. "Just look at her and smile. If there's one thing I know about Elin, it's that she's quite comfortable with the sound of silence." Flora hurried to her own room put on her clean gray plaid skirt and pin-striped blouse waist. As she brushed her hair, she wished it were still the blonde of her youth rather than a toasty brown that turned darker with each passing year.

Within minutes she and Papa, Toby, and Elin were headed down Stewart Avenue, joined by Mr. and Mrs. Pinchin, their son Henry, and his younger brother William. Conversation flowed freely among them. When they reached town, several others joined them. The Harrises, Joseph Marew, John Meehan, and Thomas Young who inquired about his cat. The congenial throng proceeded up the hill to the track. With Toby and Elin at ease in each other's company, Flora walked ahead, receiving several compliments on the tarts she had sold and many requests to sell them again soon.

Approaching the track, a voice called out to her. It was the easily recognizable voice of a longtime family friend, Big Toby Chandler. She spotted the tall, blond fellow waving at her and making his way through the crowd.

She waved back, and a moment later the handsome young man stood before her, his expression one of excitement beyond the anticipation of a mere horse race.

"Miss Flora, I was hopin' you'd be here. I've gotta ask you something."

Before she could even inquire as to his question, he blurted it out.

"May I have the honor of escorting you to the ball? Mrs. Harris says that everybody who's anybody is gonna be there. Will you go with me? Please?"

Flora smiled. "Yes, Big Toby, I'll go with you."

He gave a little jump for joy. "Thanks, Miss Flora! Thanks! We're gonna have such a good time!" Then as quickly as he'd come, he turned to go.

"Big Toby, wait. You do know how to dance, don't you?"

He answered over his shoulder. "Mrs. Harris is teaching me. I've gotta go. I've gotta tell her that you're going to the ball with me."

"See you later, Big Toby."

Flora smiled to herself, wondering how the evening would go as the partner of this fellow in his late twenties who had never developed mentally or emotionally beyond the age of fifteen. She simply must trust the Lord to bring a pleasant experience to all who would attend the ball.

Her thoughts on the horse race again, she saw that off to one side, Henry Pinchin, Thomas Young, Joseph Marew, John Meehan, and others were placing wagers. Another familiar voice, this time that of Sven Jorgensen, caught her attention.

"I am surprised to see you here, Miss McAdams."

"Why is that?" She looked up through the notch in the brim of her straw hat.

Hands on his hips, he asked, "Is not horse racing cruel, with all the whipping?"

Flora laughed. "It's the cracking of the whip above the horse's head that urges him on. And the horses love the exercise. It's good for them, don't you agree, Mr. Jorgensen? Besides, look at all the fun people are having."

He nodded.

"But I don't agree with the betting that takes place. You haven't been placing wagers, have you, Mr. Jorgensen?"

He looked her straight in the eyes, his own gleaming. "As to horses, I will not say. But I do have a bet riding on a taffy tart. I look forward to seeing it pay."

"It will, I assure you, Mr. Jorgensen. The next time I bake up a batch, I'll bring you one as promised." She turned away.

The sulkies were nearly at the starting line, preparing to race. A hush fell over the two hundred or so onlookers, then a shot rang out and the horses trotted off. Dr. Bellows' horse, Bob, took a small lead into the first turn. T. J. Streeter's horse, Frank, caught up and ran slightly ahead to the finish with a time of 1:24. The second race reversed the results with Bob finishing at 1:26 and Frank close behind. The two trotters lined up for the third and final race. Frank took the lead into the first turn on the inside.

Dr. Bellows' Bob followed closely on the outside.

Suddenly, out of nowhere, a small black dog charged at the wheel of Bob's sulky, barking and biting at it.

Bob veered sharply. The rig tilted up on one wheel.

The dog ran underneath.

Flora gasped.

The wheel touched down on the dog's leg.

Yelps cut the air.

Flora's heart stopped.

Bob raced on, leaving the dog in a cloud of dust.

Lifting her skirt, Flora ran toward the fallen creature.

CHAPTER 5

The dog lay on the track, panting heavily and whimpering, his left front leg limp and bleeding. Flora knelt beside him. This white-footed black dog had been one of the two fighting over melons and beans earlier today. She spoke quietly, reluctant to touch him.

"Good glory, you're having a rough day, aren't you, boy?"

Dr. Bellows appeared at her side. With one look, he made his diagnosis. "His leg is broken—a compound fracture. You can see the bone just inside the wound." He glanced over his shoulder at the gathering crowd. "Does anybody know whose dog this is?"

George Harris, owner of the market, eased forward. "He's a stray. I've seen him snooping around my place looking for handouts."

Frank Brinks, the proprietor of a saloon just outside the village, harrumphed. "Shoot him. The only good dog in this town is a dead one."

"No!" Flora cried. How could anyone, even a rough, tough fellow like Brinks, be so cruel?

Dr. Bellows' gaze met hers. "If this dog survives, he belongs to you. He's in bad shape right now. Are you up to the responsibility?"

Flora nodded.

"We can't move him until we stabilize his leg. We don't want the bone to come out through the wound." Turning to the crowd again, he said, "Would somebody please fetch a stick that I could use for a splint?"

Papa headed for a copse of trees outside the track, but moments later it was Sven who handed the good doctor a small but sturdy branch.

Dr. Bellows broke it to size and carefully laid it alongside the injured leg. "I need something to bind the leg to the splint."

Flora lifted the hem of her skirt. "I'll tear a length of cotton from my petticoat."

A staying hand stopped her. She gazed up into Sven's gray eyes.

"No need." With a yank on his sleeve, he ripped it from his shirt and offered it to Dr. Bellows.

He thanked Sven and skillfully wrapped the dog's broken leg. Then he shed his jacket and spread it on the ground. When he had carefully lifted the injured mutt onto his coat, he turned to the crowd.

"The races are over for tonight. I've got work to do." To Flora, he said, "Carry this poor fellow to my place and give him a few drops of Powers and Weightman Sulphate of Morphine. He's starting to go into shock. I'll be there as soon as I've put away my horse and rig."

She started to lift the trembling, whimpering patient from the track, but again, Sven's hand stopped her.

He knelt beside her and ever so gently cradled the dog in his arms.

Why did he care about this stray dog? He'd been highly annoyed when Stubby had wandered into the Machine Shop earlier. Her question would have to wait. Right now, she must get the patient to Dr. Bellows' house.

Sven at her side, they headed down the hill. As the crowd disbursed, she caught sight of Toby and Elin leaving together, and conversation flowing between them.

Along the way to Dr. Bellows', fellows from Lindbergs' boarding house took playful jabs at Sven, teasing him about his missing sleeve and the stray dog in his arms, and making suppositions about his friendship with Flora.

He teased back, sometimes in English, other times in Norwegian, but always leaving his detractors without a retort.

When they reached Dr. Bellows' place, Flora led Sven into the back room that sometimes served as a small animal surgery, and asked him to lay the dog on the table. He helped her to hold the dog's mouth open while she administered the sulphate of morphine. Soon, the whimpers and whines faded away and the dog slept.

Sven headed for the door. "I go now. I pray the dog recovers."

"Wait!" Flora came to stand before him. "Thank you. For the splint and the sleeve and for carrying the dog here. You've been such good help. But why? After the way you acted this morning, I thought you disliked dogs." She searched the angles of his face for under-standing, yet his expression remained unrevealing.

"Why indeed?" Quickly, he left.

Baffled by an answer that made no sense, she turned her attention to her patient and began to remove the binding from the injured leg. She fetched a bucket of water and a clean rag, removed the splint, cleansed the broken leg, and wiped the dust from as much of the dog's body as was practical.

When she had finished, she dumped out the dirty water and filled the bucket again to set the sleeve of Sven's shirt to soaking. Then she sat beside her patient, her hand resting lightly on his broken leg, her eyes closed.

"Almighty God, maker of heaven and earth, and all creatures that wander therein, I know that not even a fallen sparrow can escape your notice. Please, place your healing hand on this poor dog and return him to full health. Thank you, Lord. In Jesus' name, Amen."

Having done all she could until Dr. Bellows' arrival, she reached for a medical book lying on a nearby shelf and began searching for information on the human skeleton. Perhaps the bones in the forearm of a human bore resemblance to the bones in the forelegs of a dog.

~~~

Leaving Flora with her patient, Sven headed for his boarding house to change shirts. Then he set out for the livery stable where Dr. Bellows kept his horse and rig. En route, Sven tried to convince himself that he harbored no real concern for the scruffy, injured animal that lay on the good doctor's table. It made no sense to go and offer help at the stable so that the doctor could get home more quickly to treat a stray, he reasoned. Better for the stray to come to his end and leave the town with one less nuisance. But such logic played no part in his actions tonight. Memories of a dog from a distant time and place guided his conduct, and he seemed helpless to counter their influence.

~~~

"Feel of the good leg right here, Flora. Can you feel two bones?" Dr. Bellows asked.

Flora placed her hands on the dog's foreleg and felt the structure beneath the skin. "Are those the radius and the ulna?" She named the forearm bones she had seen in the diagram of the human skeleton.

"I'm no veterinarian, but I have to assume they are. Now look closely at the injured leg. Those two bones snapped off clean right here where the open wound is."

Flora nodded. "What do we do now?"

"I think we should amputate at the humerus." He indicated a point at the top of the foreleg. "The dog will probably be fine in a couple of weeks."

Flora's heart squeezed. "But he'd have only three legs for the rest of his life. Can't we save the leg?"

"We'd have to use a splint and I don't think it will work with a dog." Dr. Bellows drew a deep breath. "With people, you tell them, even young children, that they aren't to put their weight on a broken leg. Then you give them a set of crutches and you make them understand the importance of using them. But how do you give a dog crutches and tell him not to put weight on one of his four legs? And how do you keep him from chewing off the splint when you're not with him?"

Flora could think of no reasonable answers.

"Right now, my main concern is infection. If we save the leg today, I think infection is going to eventually lead to gangrene and amputation."

Considering the alternatives, it seemed that amputation was the dog's best hope for survival. Flora pushed aside her resistance. "Tell me what to do to assist with the amputation."

"First, we need to shave and disinfect the area where we'll make the incision, then . . ."

CHAPTER 6

When the incision had been stitched up, Flora helped Dr. Bellows clean up the back room. She wrung out Sven's shirtsleeve and lay it aside to dry, then used the bucket, soap, and a mop to clean the floor. When she had finished beneath the table, she stood and paused to observe the patient who was still under a heavy dose of morphine. She turned to Dr. Bellows.

"I can't help thinking how unnecessary all of this was."

"Unnecessary, or unfortunate?"

"Unnecessary. We have too many strays in this town. They get into all manner of trouble and cause themselves hurt all the time because they don't have someone who cares about them."

"Except you." Dr. Bellows grinned.

"Yes, but it's a sure thing I can't become the owner of every stray wandering Fayette. I keep thinking there must be a better way, a way to keep from having all these puppies that grow up to be adult dogs that beg from door to door and get into fights."

"And tangles with sulkies."

"That, too."

Dr. Bellows tossed his soiled rag into a basin to soak, leaned against the table, and rubbed his bearded. "Maybe dog owners should do like farmers. When a farmer has a bull that isn't needed for breeding stock, he turns it into an ox. If a dog owner has a male dog, a mutt, for instance, that isn't needed for breeding, a little surgery could keep that dog from fathering pups."

Flora's eyes widened. "That's it! Fix the male dogs so they don't make puppies. It's just that simple!"

"In theory. Getting folks to go along with the idea is another matter entirely," Dr. Bellows warned.

"But no one cares about the strays. If all of the male strays were prevented from fathering puppies, that would help."

"It would be a start. But someone would have to be willing to put the time and effort into performing the surgeries and caring for the recovering patients. Is all of that worthwhile for dogs that no one owns, just to turn them back out onto the street to fend for themselves?"

Flora considered the situation. "No. It's not practical unless the dog will have a home, and like I said, I certainly can't take in all the strays myself." She continued to ponder the problem while she went on with her mopping. By the time she had emptied the dirty water and hung up the mop, she had come up with an idea.

"Dr. Bellows, when our patient has healed from the amputation, will you please teach me how to do the surgery on him that will keep him from fathering pups? That way, if other male strays come my way, and I'm able to find homes for them, I could perform the surgeries myself."

The doctor nodded. "Give this fellow a couple of weeks, till his stitches come out. Then we'll do the operation." He took a small empty bottle from his cupboard, poured a few drops of the sulphate of morphine into it and gave it to Flora. "You can take your patient home now. When he wakes up, if he seems to be in pain, give him a few more drops of medicine. He should be up and around soon, learning how to balance on three legs, but don't let him get too active until his incision is well healed. We don't want to take the chance of splitting it open."

"I'll keep him on a leash when I take him outside." Carefully, she started to lift the dog from the table.

"Do you want this?" Dr. Bellows held up the shirtsleeve that belonged to Sven.

Flora nodded. "I'll see that it gets returned to its owner." She tucked it into her skirt pocket, then took the injured dog into her arms.

Though darkness had fallen, the starry sky and the lights showing through windows lit the way. Stubby greeted her at her front door. Mama, Papa, and Grandma were in conversation in Grandma's room at the back of the house.

Stubby followed her as she carried the slumbering dog upstairs to her bedroom and settled him on an old towel on the floor next to her bed. Stubby sniffed the stray from head to tail, paying special attention to his wound, then lay down beside him.

Two pair of footsteps rose on the stairs, a knock sounded on her open door, then Papa and Mama greeted her in turn.

"How did it go at Dr. Bellows'?"

"I see you've brought home a new patient."

Flora nodded. "Come see."

Mama gasped at the sight of the amputation.

Papa's expression turned grave. "Will he survive?"

Flora shrugged. "As Grandma would say, only time will tell. Dr. Bellows thinks he'll be in fairly good shape in a couple of weeks."

Mama wrapped Flora in a quick hug. "He's blessed to have you nursing him. I wish you success. And I wish the horse racing in this town would stop. But I don't suppose the sacrifice of one dog's leg is going to change that."

Papa gave Mama a sharp look. "You know it won't, Mary, but you're entitled to your convictions on the matter."

Through the open bedroom window came the hungry meow of the yellow cat out back.

"Mama, would you please sit with my new patient for a minute while I feed the cat?"

Mama moved toward the door. "I'll feed the cat. You tend the dog."

"Thanks, Mama."

Papa followed Mama toward the door. "It's getting late. I'd better turn in. I hope your brother won't be out too much longer. He's at Lindbergs'."

"Still talking with Elin?"

Papa shrugged. "Either he's talking with Elin or with the boarders over there."

"That reminds me." Flora reached into her pocket to produce the sleeve from Sven's shirt. "I'd better hang this up to dry. Good night, Papa." She kissed his cheek.

"Good night."

~~~

Two days later
Friday afternoon, September 5

Mama ushered the new teachers into the parlor. "Miss Ruggles, Mr. Mason, allow me to introduce you to my mother, Mrs. Ferguson, and my daughter, Flora. Mother, Flora, meet Miss Ruggles and Mr. Mason, our teachers."

Once handshakes were exchanged and seats taken in the parlor, it was evident to Flora that the young, sweet, fair-haired Lillian Ruggles seldom took her gaze off of the tall, dashing, and mustached Charles Mason whose dark hair divided flawlessly at a center part.

Mama poured the tea and passed the tarts Flora had baked fresh that afternoon.

With his first bite, Mr. Mason complimented Flora profusely on the tarts. Miss Ruggles' reaction was favorable but far more subdued.

Conversation turned to the accommodations Mr. Mason enjoyed at the hotel, compliments of Jackson Iron Company; the daily drive to town by Miss Ruggles from her parents' nearby farm; and events of the first week of school. But Flora's mind wandered to Pet. He was improving steadily from his leg amputation, yet through the parlor's open windows, she could hear him whining faintly in his pen in the back yard. Even though the whine was for attention and not from pain or hunger or thirst, Flora nevertheless longed to be with him rather than in the parlor with two teachers.

Her thoughts returned to the guests when Mama, Grandma, and Lillian Ruggles broke into laughter.

Mama's gaze turned to Flora. "Imagine one of our school children telling Mr. Mason that the founder of our town, Mr. Fayette Brown, is the Governor of Michigan."

"I can't imagine." Flora gave a nervous laugh.

Mr. Mason smiled, his gaze shifting to the taffy tarts. "Now, if I may, I surely would enjoy another one of these fine tarts you baked, Miss McAdams."

"By all means." Flora passed the tray.

Grandma smiled at Mr. Mason. "Flora baked those tarts from a special family recipe."

Flora bit her lip, praying Grandma would not launch into the story of how the tarts had played an important role in matchmaking for both Mama and Lavinia before they were married.

Mr. Mason bit into his second tart. "Mm. I've tasted no tart finer than these, and that's a fact."

Warmth rushed to Flora's cheeks. "I'm glad you like them."

Miss Ruggles' gaze momentarily shifted from Charles to Flora. "I'd be ever so thankful if you would write out the recipe for me. I'd like to bake a batch of these taffy tarts myself."

"No need to write it out," said Grandma. "It's simple enough." In less than a minute, she had explained the procedure.

Shortly afterward, teacups empty and conversation at an end, Mr. Mason and Miss Ruggles expressed their thanks to Mama and headed for the door. As Mama saw them out, she said, "Now if ever either of you is ill, God forbid, and needs someone to take your class temporarily, I'll be glad to serve as a substitute."

Mr. Mason smiled. "Thank you kindly for your offer, Mrs. McAdams, but I'm healthy as a May morning. Can't remember the last time I was sick a-bed."

Lillian nodded. "Neither can I remember the last time I was sick. But we'll keep your offer in mind. Again, thank you for your hospitality, and for your recipe. Good day."

The moment the front door closed behind them, Flora hurried out the back door to let Pet out of his pen for affection and exercise.

CHAPTER 7

The next morning beneath a cloudless blue sky, Flora headed out to the back yard, a bowl of breakfast scraps in one hand and a bowl of water in the other. Stubby came alongside, sniffing at the provisions.

Flora looked him directly in the eyes. "Stubby, go lie down. You've already had your breakfast."

Obediently, he retreated to his place beneath the shade tree, lying down with a sigh while she carried the bowls toward the pen where her healing amputee lay waiting. Long before she got there, Pet's tail wagged in wide sweeps. She opened the gate and set the bowls inside his pen. With little effort, he balanced on his three legs and lowered his head to eat with gusto.

While he was eating, she took a close look at his incision. It was healing well, and still no sign of infection had appeared. She whispered thanks to God that within days she would be able to remove the stitches.

When Pet had finished eating and drinking, she tied a leash to the collar she had made for him of braided twine and began walking him around the yard. Stubby joined them. To Flora's surprise, Pet began to pull in the direction of the cage she had used for the cat that had passed his hairball and been returned to Thomas Young the day before. She allowed Pet to thoroughly sniff the cage until his curiosity was satisfied, then they continued on their route. When they came to the chicken coop, he whined and started to paw at the chicken wire. In a flash, he lost his balance and came down on his incision with a blood-curdling yelp.

He lay in the dirt, licking his wound and whining softly while Stubby edged close to inspect.

Flora's stomach soured as she knelt beside Pet. She pushed Stubby out of the way and began to examine Pet's wound. No further damage was visible. She whispered a prayer of thanks and carefully picked up the hurting creature, returned him to his pen, removed his leash, and sat with him until his pain subsided. When he was resting comfortably, she went in the house to get the list of supplies she needed, a market basket, and her money. Then, she headed for the company store, Stubby at her side. He lay down outside the store while she went in to shop.

Just inside the door, a parlor stove had been put on display with a sign.

Win this stove!
Raffle to be held at the ball on Oct. 3.
Buy your tickets here.
10 cents each or 3 for 25 cents.

Flora smiled. Papa was right. It hadn't taken long for someone to plan a raffle at the ball. She paused a moment to inspect the stove, a Round Oak model from Dowagiac, a Lower Peninsula town. It was a fine stove, to be sure, both practical and attractive.

She moved on to purchase her supplies. Down the aisle, the store clerk, her neighbor and friend Henry Pinchin, was assisting Mary Caffey, the servant to the furnace foreman's family who lived in their neighborhood. In fact, Henry was so attentive to the auburn-haired girl, he almost didn't acknowledge Flora's greeting to them both when she passed them on her way to the counter.

She had set her basket down and was gazing longingly at the big glass jar of horehound drops when Mr. Powell came out from the back room greeting her with gusto.

"Good morning, Miss McAdams! Fine day we're having, is it not?"

"Fine, indeed, Mr. Powell." She handed him her list. "I hope I can purchase these items for eighty cents. I need them badly and that's all the money I have to my name." He read the list, stroked his chin, and then smiled. "I think eighty cents will cover it. Let me get your order together. We'll add it up." He whistled softly while gathering her supplies.

Flora browsed the millinery. A new straw hat would look more fetching than the one she was wearing, with the notch a cat had nibbled. But a new hat would have to wait until another day. She had left the millinery and moved on to the yard goods counter when the door opened with a jingle and Sven walked in.

He greeted her with a nod. "How is the dog?"

"Recovering nicely. Thank you for asking."

He moved on and then paused at the display of men's shirts marked "CLEARANCE SALE."

In a flash, Flora recalled the shirtsleeve that still hung over the towel bar of her wash stand.

"Mr. Jorgensen, I have the sleeve of your shirt. If you'll bring me the rest of it, I'll see that the shirt is repaired."

"I'll bring it." Sven turned to Henry Pinchin, inquired about a new corn broom needed at the Machine Shop, and took his leave.

A minute later Mr. Powell returned to Flora. "Your order is ready, Miss McAdams. I'll tally the bill." He added a column of figures he had written alongside the items on her list. "It comes to ninety cents. Would you be interested in a raffle ticket today? I could charge twenty cents to your father's account."

"No raffle ticket for me, thank you, and no charges to Papa's account." She studied the prices written on her list, set aside the comb with which she had planned to groom her patients, and began filling her basket.

Mr. Powell assisted, thanking her for her patronage and bidding her good day.

She stepped outside and called to Stubby. "Come on, boy. Time to go home and check on Pet." She started up the street. When Stubby didn't come alongside, she looked back. He hadn't even stirred.

"Stubby! Come!" Her voice was clearly audible above the clatter of wagons and the clang of hammers on iron at the casting house.

He ignored her still, not even lifting his head.

Flora's stomach sank to her knees. She hurried back to Stubby, bent down, and cupped her hand over his nose.

Not a breath stirred.

"Stubby! Oh, Stubby!" She dropped to her knees and wrapped her arms about his lifeless body.

CHAPTER 8

With supper over and the dishes put away, Flora and her family gathered near Stubby's favorite tree in the back yard. Papa and Toby heaped fresh dirt alongside a rectangular pit. Nearby, an old quilt concealed his remains. The fellows set shovels aside and carefully lowered Flora's beloved pet into the grave.

Flora struggled to hold back her tears, but her effort was futile. Grandma gave her a consoling hug and Mama handed her a dry handkerchief. Flora blotted the moisture from her cheeks and bowed her head while Papa prayed.

"Almighty God, we thank Thee for the joy that Your creature Stubby brought us for so many years. We give him back to You now, committing his body to the ground, earth to earth, ashes to ashes, dust to dust. Bring us consolation over our loss, and special comfort to Flora in her time of sorrow. Thank you. In the name of Your son, Jesus, we pray. Amen."

Papa and Toby, wet-faced and grim, reached for their shovels. The first load of dirt hit the grave and sent Flora into another round of sobs. Mama pulled her close. Flora closed her eyes and wept into her shoulder. When she opened her eyes again, Papa and Toby had finished their task and were headed toward the house with Grandma.

Flora gazed up at Mama and struggled for composure. "I just want to be alone for awhile and . . ." Her throat constricted, cutting off her words.

Mama nodded, dabbed the tears from her own cheeks, and went inside.

Flora sat beneath the tree. The fresh grave brought to mind the days of Stubby's youth. Back then, she'd had to tie him to the tree to prevent him from running off. In his boredom he had often dug holes of his own in the very place where he now lay buried, and the shovels that had dug his grave had filled his unwanted hollows.

She remembered, too, the day she had forgotten to tie him outside before going off to her friends' house to play. The destruction he had caused in her bedroom, tearing apart the new doll Grandma, Mama, and her sister Lavinia had sewn for her and chewing on the doll-sized rocking chair hand-carved by Huck, her brother-in-law, had made Flora wish she'd never known the pup. But within a couple of days, her anger had passed and he had begun to work his way back into her heart.

Out of habit Flora reached out, expecting to feel Stubby's sleek copper coat beneath her hand. She sobbed out loud. The affectionate canine that had served as her greatest playmate, her best friend, her loyal confidante, and her fierce protector was forever gone from this earth. No more would she feel the nudge of his cold nose against her arm begging for attention, or see the love in his warm brown eyes when he looked up at her. She would never again smell the oil in his coat that had given him his own, unique essence or sense the comfort and security that the scent of him had brought to her life. No longer would he walk the village streets with her or the path along the limestone bluff. He would not be waiting for her outside the store when she shopped or at the garden when she picked vegetables. And he would not be there to investigate the hurting creatures brought to her for healing.

She buried her face in her handkerchief and cried softly. Mingled with her sobs was the whimpering of Pet but she ignored the sound, missing Stubby and his wet kisses that had always washed away her tears. So vivid was her memory that she could feel him now, nudging her with his wet nose. The sense of him was so keen she was compelled to look up.

Her gaze met that of Pet, who began to lap away her salty tears with such enthusiasm, she couldn't help but laugh.

"How did you get loose?" She took the insistent mutt into her arms and hugged him. And then she discovered Sven standing near Pet's kennel.

He approached her, shirt in hand, and Flora remembered the promise she had made to reattach the sleeve. But all she could think about was the small, tail-wagging dog who refused to let her tears fall. Half laughing, half crying, she gazed up at Sven.

"Can you believe that all I have left is this crazy little dog who doesn't even know enough to stay off the race track?"

Sven smiled. He sat beside her, his quiet presence comforting. And when Pet had thoroughly chased Flora's tears away, Sven welcomed the dog's affection, allowing him to lick his face. Soon, the dog settled between them. Words seemed unnecessary as they sat together, Flora petting the dog's head, Sven stroking his side. Once, her hand brushed against Sven's.

"Sorry," she blurted, but his upturned mouth assured her there had been no need for an apology. She reached for the shirt in need of repair. "I'll get this back to you soon."

"No rush." His hand moved slowly along Pet's side and hindquarters.

~~~

Sven couldn't help thinking about Tigger, the dog he had loved in Norway, and the anguish of leaving his faithful pal behind on the day the ship departed. His Norwegian elkhound had been shut up in the barn but somehow had gotten free and raced to the shore, arriving on the dock at the very moment the steamer cast off. Barking frantically, Tigger raced along the shore, every now and then, pausing to sit back and let loose a heart-rending howl.

For a mile, Tigger followed, coming to a promontory where the steamer passed close by. Sven shouted to Tigger, commanding him to go home. But at the sound of his master's voice, Tigger jumped off the promontory into the icy water of the fiord.

Sven's heart plummeted, sinking to the very depths along with his loyal pet. Then Tigger's head bobbed to the surface. Sven's hope renewed, he again commanded the dog to go home. Then the hound's head dipped below the surface, never to rise again.

The vision had haunted Sven for weeks. Thoughts of Tigger now rent anew the old wound of his parting. It was the distant memory of him that prompted Sven to help save this little black dog's life. How well Sven understood the sorrow of Flora McAdams. He prayed that her new little dog could bring her comfort.

~~~

As quietly as Sven had come, he took his leave, glancing back to tip his brown plush hat and then disappearing from sight.

He had been gone but a moment when Elin came to sit with Flora. The look of sympathy in Elin's kind, blue eyes, her gentle hug, and her quiet presence brought needed comfort.

As the sun sank below the treetops and the nighthawks began to circle, Flora couldn't help thinking that her beloved Stubby would share these moments with her no more. Tears seeped from her eyes, and even Pet with all his pluck could not wash the sorrow away with his eager tongue. Her head was downcast, her mind on the fresh grave when a familiar voice came to her.

"Flora McAdams, you have work to do!"

Dr. Bellows came toward her with a large tan dog on a leash. Pet barked frantically, standing firm on his three legs in an effort to protect his mistress from the perceived foes. Flora scooped him into her arms and managed to quiet his loud barks to low growls.

Dr. Bellows continued. "This dog needs surgery. He's been roaming the streets, bothering the female dogs of one of my patients. I'll teach you how to neuter him."

Flora wiped the dampness from her cheeks. "Not tonight, Dr. Bellows. I just couldn't."

"Why not?" he demanded somewhat gruffly.

Flora's gaze traveled to Stubby's grave.

Dr. Bellows' voice softened. "I heard about Stubby and I'm sorry about your loss, but you've had all day to cry about him. If he were here right now, what do you think he'd want you to do? Sit there and cry some more, or get up and do something about the dog problem in this town?"

Half-laughing, half-crying, Flora got up, put Pet in his kennel, bid goodnight to Elin, and went with Dr. Bellows.

CHAPTER 9

Two days later

Flora wiped loose dirt off the fresh tomatoes, summer squash, cucumbers, pickles, and melons she had picked early that morning, set several aside for Mama and Grandma, placed the remainder in two baskets, and started for Harris's market. Pet and Big Boy, the dog she had neutered with Dr. Bellows' help, protested being left behind with loud barks and yelps, but she ignored them, having already walked both dogs around Cedar Lane and seen to their needs for food and water.

She smiled to herself, listening to the deep, chesty bark of Big Boy. From the sound of him and the way he acted, no one would guess that the night before last he had undergone surgery. He not only had recovered from the operation, but also had learned to sit and lie down on command. He was eager to please and would make a nice pet for someone, if indeed Flora could find one soul in all of Fayette who would take on this large dog.

She would worry about that later. Now, she needed to sell fresh produce and replenish her animal welfare fund. The bells on the market door jingled when she entered. Joseph Marew looked up from the hindquarter of beef he was trimming and said hello, then George Harris called out from somewhere in the back room.

"I'll be right with you."

Flora began arranging her produce on the countertop. She had nearly finished when George came out front.

"Good morning, Flora. I see you've been to your garden already this morning. Fine looking vegetables you've got there."

"Thank you, George." She set out the last tomato and turned to face her him. He wore furrowed brows instead of his usual smile, and tucked into the butcher apron tied at his waist was a hammer. "What's that for? Are you using a new method of tenderizing beef?"

He laughed half-heartedly. "Not quite. Somebody broke in here last night and stole my new rifle. I've been trying to piece the rear door back together. You haven't seen anyone carrying a Winchester repeater over their shoulder, have you?"

Flora shook her head. "Any idea who could have done it?"

George offered a puzzled look. "Could be anyone who's walked in here since I bought the rifle a month ago. Everybody could see it when I had the door to the back room opened. That was nearly every day last month to get a breeze through the place."

Flora thought a moment. "Was that the rifle you were bragging about when you told some fellows you'd shoot the hats off them next time you saw them at the rifle range?"

He chuckled. "That's the one. But when did you hear me say that?"

"About a month ago when I was here to get a bone for Stubby. Mr. Brinks and Mr. Schiling were in here at the time. And John Meehan and a man I'd never seen before."

George thought a moment. "Schiling's moved on. Brinks has been pretty busy running that saloon east of here. John Meehan is honest as the day is long. Guess I don't recall the other fellow." He turned to Joseph. "Do you remember who was here that day?"

Joseph shook his head. "Sorry, boss. John would know. He has a mind like a bear trap."

"I hope you find the thief, George," Flora said with all sincerity. "And I hope you sell all my produce today. I sure could use the money."

"Check back just before I close and we'll settle up. I'll save a bone for that new little dog of yours, too. Sorry about old Stubby."

"Thanks. See you later." She headed for home. The sun sparkled on the water, and a refreshing breeze came in from the north, but like the gray cloud that hung low near the horizon, the thought troubled her that a thief was afoot in Fayette—a thief who had chosen a rifle as his plunder. Break-ins were unheard-of in this town, and crime so rare that a jail had not been built until this year, and hadn't seen an inmate yet.

When she arrived at her back yard, Pet and Big Boy competed with each other to see who could bark louder.

Pet was no match for the larger dog. Then a thought struck Flora. Tying a leash to Big Boy, she took him out of his kennel and headed back to town. She was passing the hotel when Big Toby came from around back.

"Miss Flora! Miss Flora! Wait up!" He hurried toward her.

She paused beside the road, commanding Big Boy to sit, and holding tight to his leash lest he grow wary of Big Toby as he approached. But the dog showed no sign of apprehension, and licked furiously when Big Toby held out his hand for the dog to sniff.

"He likes you, Toby. Maybe you should have a dog of your own—this dog!"

"Mr. Harris would never let me," Toby said, and Flora remembered that he bunked in the hotel dormitory where pets were not allowed. Then, he focused on her, his blue eyes bright with expectation. "Don't forget the ball. You're still going with me, aren't you?"

"Of course I am. Have you been practicing your dance steps?"

"Every day with Mrs. Harris. She's teaching Miss Phillips how to dance, too." He referred to Mrs. Harris's middle-aged maid.

With one last pat of Big Boy's head, Big Toby bid Flora good bye and dashed off.

She continued toward her destination, entering Harris's market with Big Boy. George stood up from his desk behind the counter. "Who's that handsome fellow you're with? Can't be Stubby's replacement. You've already got that little dog with three legs. Or did you decide it will take two dogs to replace old Stubby?"

Flora shook her head. "This is Big Boy. He was a stray. He needs a home. I thought this would be just the place for him. He'll burglar-proof your store so you won't have to worry about anyone stealing from you again."

George shook his head. "Can't have a dog in here with all the meat I handle."

"Keep him out back during the day. Then, when all your meat is put away in the locker at night, let him inside until morning. He'll chase off intruders, guaranteed."

George grew thoughtful.

Flora prayed.

George's head began moving from side to side. "No. I can't do it. Now if that were a hunting dog, maybe I'd give it some thought. But that bruiser would really eat into my profits."

"I don't know what you paid for that Winchester repeater, but it seems to me it would take an awful long time for Big Boy to cost you that much in food, since he's perfectly happy with table scraps."

George stared at the dog, then shook his head again. "I just don't think it's a good idea, a dog at a meat market."

"Let me know if you change your mind." Flora led Big Boy out the door.

Wagons clattered past, startling Big Boy. He lunged, barked, and growled. It was all Flora could do to keep him from dragging her down the street. She was still struggling for control when Frank Brinks drove up.

"Hello, Miss McAdams. Quite a dog ya got there."

His voice set Big Boy into another round of barks and growls. Flora held onto the rope leash with all her might and verbally reassured the dog. She nearly had him calmed down when Brinks jumped off his wagon and came toward her.

The hair on Big Boy's back stood up as the towering, scar-faced man approached. Big Boy lunged at Brinks, baring his teeth and growling viciously. Flora held the leash with both hands and dug in her heels.

Brinks stayed out of reach, shouting to Flora above Big Boy's barking. "I could sure use a pair of dogs similar to that one. I hear you're takin' in strays and fixin' 'em. My dogs don't need no surgery, but they oughta be matched in size and sex. Know where I could find a couple of studs or bitches with big chests?"

Struggling to hold the rope fast, and to be heard, Flora shouted her reply. "Not at the moment, but there are so many strays in this town, it shouldn't take long to find what you want."

"You look around for me, will ya? I'll make it worth your time. And I'll check back with ya in a few days." He climbed aboard his wagon and drove off.

When Big Boy finally calmed down and began walking nicely by her side, Flora grew excited at the prospect of locating two strays for an eager owner. She didn't particularly care for Brinks and his rough ways, but at least two homeless dogs would be getting regular meals and someone to look after them.

That didn't solve the problem of a home for Big Boy. Taking on two challenges at once, she began to canvas the town looking for a new owner for Big Boy, and inquiring about strays that would fit Brinks' description.

~~~

Several hours later, having been unsuccessful in finding Big Boy a new home, or locating dogs for Brinks, Flora hurried down Stewart Avenue toward town. Within moments the five o'clock whistle would blow, signaling the end of the day shift and the end of business hours for George Harris. She prayed he would have good news for her concerning the sale of her garden produce. She desperately needed *something* to go right today. The difficulty of finding a home for Big Boy she could understand, but the lack of appropriate strays puzzled her. It was almost as if all the larger dogs in town had taken to the woods for the day in anticipation of her search. She would have continued her efforts in the afternoon if not for Mama reminding her that she must repair Sven's shirt.

Twice, she set in the sleeve, only to find that her seam had puckered and must be ripped out. After removing the last set of stitches, time and patience had come to an end. How was it that she could sew up an injured dog, but not a ripped shirt?

She had handed the shirt and sleeve to Mama asking for her help. Thankfully, Mama was perfectly willing to make the repair, but only if Flora promised to practice her dance steps with Papa after supper so that she would be ready for the ball.

When Flora had pointed out that the ball was still three- and-a-half weeks away, Mama had said, "Better to start too early than too late. Now, do you want my help with Mr. Jorgensen's shirt, or not?"

"Yes, please, Mama. Dance lessons tonight," Flora replied with a sigh.

The exchange left Flora wishing she had never mentioned in the course of lunch conversation that Big Toby was practicing his dancing with Mrs. Harris. Flora did not relish the thought of an evening spent struggling for grace and elegance to the rhythm of dance music.

The steam whistle sounded, blasting that thought from her mind and speeding her steps to Harris's. She dashed into the market, running headlong into George, who was about to close and lock the door.

CHAPTER 10

Flora's collision with George Harris knocked a key out of his hand and halfway across the floor.

She scooped it up from the floor and held it out to him. "So sorry, George. I guess I was in too big of a hurry to get here before you closed."

He smiled and took the key from her. "No harm done. It's good you came when you did. I just sold the last of your produce." He went behind the counter, reached into his cash box, and laid a half-dollar in front of her. "If you'll wait a minute, Joseph saved a couple of nice bones for your dogs."

While he wrapped them up, Flora dropped the coin into her pocket and whispered a prayer of thanks for the returns from her efforts in the garden. At least *this* part of her day had worked out the way she planned. She was day dreaming about the supplies that she would buy with the fifty cents when George placed an especially large package in front of her.

"Here you go. These ought to keep those two mutts of yours busy for a while."

"Thanks so much! And let me know if you change your mind about Big Boy."

"That reminds me. John Meehan stopped by. He remembered that day a month ago when you and Schiling and Brinks were in here. Said he could see perfectly the face of the stranger you mentioned, but hasn't crossed paths with the fellow since and has no idea who he is or where he was from."

"Guess that's not much help where your rifle is concerned. Are you *sure* you don't want me to bring you Big Boy?"

"I'm sure. Good night, Flora."

She stepped out into a street filled with tired, dirty workers happy to be heading home after a long day at the furnace. Rising up on tiptoe, she peered through the crowd in search of Papa or Toby, and instead glimpsed Sven coming her way in the company of two other Lindberg boarders. Hastily, she turned and started for home, intending to avoid any talk of the damaged shirt that was not yet repaired.

She hadn't gone far when, from behind her came a very proper sounding voice that she nonetheless recognized as Papa's.

"Miss McAdams, may I carry your books? I mean, your bones?"

Flora laughed as Papa came along one side of her, and Toby, the other.

Papa took the package from her and sniffed. "Mm. The dogs will be happy tonight."

"I'm happy tonight, too." Flora flashed her half-dollar in front of Papa and Toby.

Toby eyed the coin intently. "I don't suppose you'd consider making me a loan until payday?"

Flora dropped the half dollar into her pocket. "Good glory, no! Why do you need money?"

Toby grinned. "Just teasing. I suppose you and Elin have your evening all planned."

Flora shook her head. "I wish it were so. Instead, I'm going to be spending it with Mama and Papa learning what I'll need to do to be a picture of perfect grace and elegance at the ball on October third." She turned to Papa. "You *did* promise to help me, and Mama has planned it for this evening. I hope you don't mind."

"I can't think of a nicer way to spend my time. Except maybe . . ."

"What?" Flora demanded as they entered the back yard.

"Except maybe watching a horse race or a ball game." Toby answered for Papa. "But neither is planned for tonight."

"Spoken like a true Fayette pig iron man." Flora took the butcher package from Papa and headed for the dog kennels. While Papa and Toby washed at the well, Flora approached Pet and Big Boy with their bones, taking pleasure in the sight of their wagging tails, and their eagerness to sit and lie down in order to earn their special rewards.

She watched them enjoy their treats for a minute, then went to the well to wash up. Toby was still there. He pumped the handle while she washed hands and face in the cold, refreshing water. When she turned to go inside for supper, he restrained her, his hand on her arm. She nearly jerked away, remembering all the times when, as a small girl, she'd been subject to his teasing and his superior strength, and forced to go here or there as his prankish ways demanded. But those days were past. Now, when she turned to face him, she could read the uncertainty in his eyes.

"Flora, do you suppose it would be okay if . . . . He released her, pulled off his cap, and ran a hand through his thick hair. "About tonight. I really need dance lessons, too."

She smiled. "I'm sure Mama and Papa and Grandma will give you all the help you need. At least I won't be the sole center of their attention, clumsy as I am."

"I suppose Elin already knows everything that's needed to avoid missteps on the dance floor."

Flora shrugged. "She's never said. So she's going with you, then?"

Toby simply smiled, then headed inside for supper.

Flora had been so sad over Stubby, then so busy taking care of her two new dogs and working in the garden, that in the time she'd spent with Elin since the date for the ball had been set, the subject of dance floor skills had not come up.

When supper was over, the kitchen cleaned up, and the dogs walked, Mama gathered the family in the parlor.

"Papa, will you and Toby please move the sofa, tables, and chairs back against the walls? Mother, perhaps you can find another place for the china figurines so they won't get broken when the tables are moved. And Flora, would you please help me roll up the rug? Then, we'll start."

"But we don't have anyone to provide music," Flora observed.

Papa laughed. "What do you mean, we don't have anyone to provide music?" He hummed a reasonable rendition of a Strauss waltz.

Grandma began counting. "*One*, two, three, *one*, two three . . ."

Mama grinned. "We are all set to begin our lessons. We've got a dance floor, an orchestra, and Mother to keep time. Papa, you and I will first demonstrate how the waltz is done."

They faced each other. Papa bowed, Mama curtsied, and stepped into each other's arms. Gracefully they circled the room twice, came to a stop, then bowed and curtsied again.

Flora's head moved slowly from side to side. "I'll never be able to do it. My feet can't learn that many steps."

Mama laughed. "Nonsense. Your feet simply repeat the same pattern over and over." She offered an encouraging smile. "Let's start with something easy, the curtsey and bow. Come over here beside me. Toby, stand beside your father. We'll show you."

Moments later, the bow and curtsey mastered, Papa took Mama's hand in his. "Now it's time to learn the waltz steps."

Toby hesitated, his gaze shifting to the front window. Flora hastened to draw the lace curtains.

Still hesitant, Toby turned to Mama. "Do you have any old sheets? Anybody can see right through those lacy curtains."

"I'll get them." Flora headed for the closet.

A couple of minutes later, behind the privacy of sheet-draped windows, Papa began teaching Toby the man's steps in the waltz on one side of the parlor, while Mary taught Flora the lady's steps on the other side.

Flora watched, completely befuddled at first, but minutes later she could execute all six steps without any prompting from Mama.

Toby had also learned the steps in his routine, and Papa ushered him to Flora. "Now it's time for the two of you to practice together. Toby, hold Flora thus." He gave specific instructions as to placement and position of his hands.

Flora expected to hear a groan of protest from Toby, but instead he was all business, assuming the position Papa described.

"Excellent, Toby." Papa beamed. "Now watch your mother and me."

Slowly, Toby and Flora mimicked Mama and Papa's moves, rough at first, then with more confidence and grace as the six-step pattern took them around the room. They had completed one circle when someone knocked loudly on the front door.

Dancing ceased while Papa answered, returning immediately with Elin and an explanation. "Our neighbor came to ask if all was well. She saw the sheets at the windows and feared someone was deathly sick."

Flora laughed. "Deathly clumsy is more like it. Papa and Mama are doing their best to teach us the waltz."

"Come join us, won't you, Elin?" Mama waved her farther into the room. "Toby is getting quite good. He was just waltzing with Flora, but since you're here, there's no reason the two of you shouldn't get in some practice. Do you know the waltz?"

Elin nodded, her cheeks turning bright pink.

Toby's face grew ruddy.

Neither moved an inch toward the other.

Grandma said, "You can't practice the waltz by just standing there, gawking at one another. Go on. Forget the rest of us are here." She began to count and Papa hummed, taking up the waltz position with Flora and leading her around the room.

With a little nudge from Mama, Elin moved toward Toby. He took up the waltz position and led off, his broad shoulders making his svelte partner look even more slender. Elin easily followed, light on her feet and perfect in every step until Toby came down on her toes.

"Sorry! So sorry! Are you all right?" Toby dropped to his knees to take a close look at her foot.

Elin laughed lightly. "No harm. Shall we try again?"

Grandma slowed the tempo, Papa hummed, and again they began to dance in perfect synchronization around the floor, the tempo gradually increasing to a moderate beat.

Flora and Papa stepped off to the side to watch. How perfectly matched Elin's quiet, confident ways were to Toby's silent, sometimes uncertain manner.

When the song came to an end, Mama said, "Stay for tea, Elin?"

"Yes, thank you, Mrs. McAdams."

Grandma started toward the kitchen. "I'll fetch the tea and cookies while you folks put the parlor back in order."

With the furniture and rugs back to normal and the tea still steeping, Flora took a few minutes to give each of her dogs some water and exercise in the back yard. When she returned to the house, Grandma had the tea tray ready, and Flora carried it to the parlor for her.

After cups had been filled and cookies passed, Grandma said, "I suppose, Elin, that you're looking forward to attending the ball with Toby."

"I dream of going, ma'am. Toby has not invited me, but," she paused.

Grandma's gaze cut sharply in Toby's direction. "Haven't you asked her yet, son? What in heaven's name are you waiting for?"

Flora's heart went out to Toby, though she was as surprised as Grandma to learn that the question had not been settled. Thinking fast, she said, "I'm sure Toby meant to ask Elin last week, but something probably came up."

Grandma scowled. "Like what? A case of bashfulness?" To Toby, she said, "For goodness sake, son, ask her now."

Toby looked so horrified, Flora wasn't even sure his tongue would work. She was thankful to hear him voice the quiet, if not confident question.

"Elin, may I have the honor of escorting you to the ball?"

Elin's soft blue eyes held Toby with great tenderness. "I would like to accept, but I cannot. I'm *so* sorry. I hope we can still be friends."

Toby looked crushed, but managed to mutter, "Of course we can be friends."

Conversation turned to Elin's news of relatives en route to Fayette from Sweden, Flora's success in the garden, Grandma's new quilting project, Toby's latest catch from the bay, and the new recipe for cold catsup. Though Toby said almost nothing, his focus remained almost exclusively on Elin, and when she rose to part company, he moved quickly to usher her to the door. They were leaving the parlor when a loud, insistent knock sounded at the back door.

"Good glory! Who could that be?" Flora hurried down the hall and through the kitchen to the door at the back of Grandma's room.

On the stoop stood Sven, an anxious look on his face. "Come quick! Dog out! Big trouble!"

CHAPTER 11

Big Boy's kennel was empty. With Toby and Elin close behind, Flora followed Sven to the far side of the boarding house. There, in Mrs. Lindberg's rose garden, Big Boy was digging a sizable hole in which he evidently intended to bury the butcher bone that lay beside him. To Flora's profound dismay—and that of Mrs. Lindberg—he had already dug up three of her cherished rose bushes and was in the process of uprooting a fourth.

Mrs. Lindberg grabbed a broom. "I'll put a stop to that." She swatted the dog.

Big Boy attacked the broom, yanking it from her and tearing it apart so ferociously that all but Flora took several steps back.

"I can get him home," Flora assured the others, "but I'll need about five small cubes of cheese."

Mrs. Lindberg hurried to her kitchen, returning a minute later with the requested items.

In her absence, Big Boy had lost his fascination with the broom and resumed his digging despite Flora's vocal commands to the contrary.

Papa, Mama, Grandma, and several boarders came to see what the fuss was all about.

Big Boy ignored them all, pawing up dirt with the efficiency of a shovel.

With the cheese in her pocket, Flora gave one loud clap of her hands and said the word, "Cheese!"

Big Boy immediately stopped digging and focused intently on her. She tossed him a cheese cube.

He snatched it out of the air, gulped it down, and looked to her for more.

"Big Boy, come!"

Instantly, he loped toward her. The moment he reached her, she snapped her fingers and offered another cheese cube and praise.

She headed toward home and issued a new command. "Big Boy, heel!"

The instant she stepped off, he followed at her left side, earning another snap of her fingers, praise, and cheese reward.

Flora continued toward home, snapping her fingers and rewarding him again for staying with her even when he seemed distracted by the others following him.

When he reached his kennel, he went in on command, earning the last cheese cube and a shower of praise and affection.

Pet barked for attention, but Flora ignored him for the moment. How would she secure the chewed-off latch on Big Boy's kennel?

Toby, a length of wire in hand, quickly solved the problem.

Sven held up Big Boy's butcher bone. "What about this?"

Papa eyed it with a wry smile. "Now *that* is a real bone of contention."

Mrs. Lindberg laughed. "You can say it again."

"Now *that* is a real bone of contention."

"*And* conversation," said Mama. "Think of the stories you'll tell your grandchildren about the roses that almost died because of a silly dog bone, but were saved by five cubes of cheese from your kitchen. I'm sure the roses will live. They still have good roots."

"I'll go right now and replant them," Flora offered. "I'm so sorry, Mrs. Lindberg." To Sven, she said, "And I'd be much obliged if you'd plant that bone in the bottom of Snail-Shell Harbor."

Papa and Toby, shovels in hand, helped Flora to replant the rose bushes, complete with compost and a thorough watering, while Sven went to dispose of the bone.

When the garden work was finished, Mrs. Lindberg gave the job a good looking-over. "My roses look like nothing happened. But this broom is ruined." She bent to pick up the gnawed handle and some tufts of loose straw.

In the distance Pet sounded a hungry bark.

"I'll bring you a brand new broom tomorrow morning," Flora promised. "Now, I'd better go and feed Pet. Good night."

She headed for home, her brother and father with her. In the kitchen, she fixed two bowls of scraps for the dogs then carried them out to the kennels. When Pet had finished, she took him for a walk down Stewart Avenue. She hadn't gone far when she met Sven.

"The bone sank," he reported.

"Good riddance. Thank you."

With a nod and a smile, he began walking with her.

She gazed up at him and smiled in return, hoping he had more to say, but he remained silent until they had walked in a loop up Sheldon Avenue and back to her own yard.

Sven's focus on Big Boy, he shook his head. "If I had not seen, I would not believe. A monster dog tamed by cheese. You do a miracle."

"There's nothing miraculous about it. It's just a simple process of rewarding desired behavior."

She put Pet in his kennel. While refilling water bowls for both dogs—with help from Sven—she explained that Dr. Bellows had told her the methods of trick dog trainers. Then she described how she had used those methods with modifications of her own to train Stubby first, and now Pet and Big Boy. "So you see, there's no miracle about it, just good training."

Sven nodded, but kept his silence though his gaze remained on her. What was he thinking?

She glanced upward. "Dusk is falling. I'd better go inside. Good night."

"Wait. My shirt?"

Flora smiled. "I'll have it for you tomorrow."

"The taffy tart, too?"

"The taffy tart, too. Stop by after supper."

He touched the brim of his hat and took his leave.

Flora headed for the house, glancing back over her shoulder, and catching Sven looking back at her. She waved and went inside.

Grandma greeted her. "Out walking with that boarder from Mrs. Lindberg's, I see." She pressed a strand of silver hair toward the knot at the top of her head.

"Not exactly," Flora replied, hoping to escape Grandma's inquisition."

"But I saw the two of you bring Pet back from a walk."

"That's true, but we didn't start out together. I was already on the walk with Pet when I came across Mr. Jorgensen. He was on his way back to Lindbergs' after tossing the 'bone of contention' into the harbor. I'm happy to report that it now lies at the bottom never to be retrieved by dog or man." She started for the kitchen.

"Flora, about this Mr. Jorgensen fellow—he's sweet on you, you know."

Flora came to an abrupt halt and pivoted to face Grandma again. "I don't mean to argue, but that's impossible."

"It's God's honest truth." The corners of Grandma's mouth turned upward. "I can tell by the way he looks at you."

Flora shook her head. "With my plain face and impossible-to-find waist, he surely can't be sweet on me. What could he find to admire? I'm built more like a tree trunk than an hourglass. Surely you're mistaken."

"I am *not* mistaken. You're much more attractive than you give yourself credit for. You have a fine head on your shoulders and a crown of thick, hair like unto a

shiny chestnut. When you smile, your whole face lights
with joy, and when you laugh, it's like the music of a
stream bubbling past smooth stones. God knows that too
many of his creatures never find a time to laugh." She
leaned forward. "I've known some women with hourglass figures faces like Helen of Troy who don't know
how to laugh. As for Mr. Jorgensen, I'm certain he has
noticed *your* smiles and laughter, and a whole lot more
I've failed to mention. You have caught his fancy.
There's no doubt."

Flora grew thoughtful. Could Grandma possibly be
right? When Sven helped with Pet and sat quietly with
her after Stubby died—were those gestures ways of
showing interest in her that she had not recognized?

Mama entered the room and Flora eagerly turned to
her with another pressing matter. "Will Mr. Jorgensen's
shirt be repaired by tomorrow evening? He inquired after
it and I took the liberty of promising it would be ready."

"Then it will be."

"Thank you, Mama. I don't know what I'd do without
you!" She gave Mama a hug and started for the door.

Suddenly remembering another part of her promise to
Sven, she turned to Mama and Grandma. "Would you
two please help me bake taffy tarts tomorrow? I still owe
one to Mr. Jorgensen from the sale last week. I promised
I'd have the tart for him when he comes to pick up his
shirt after supper."

Grandma grinned. "See! I told you! Taffy tarts are a
sure sign that what I've been saying is true. The two of
you are sweet on each other."

Flora shook her head and laughed. "It's a business transaction. He paid in advance for a tart after I'd sold out, and I said I'd have it for him tomorrow."

Grandma waved her finger. "It may be business to you, but to him, it's much more. And after he tastes the tart, well, it's only a matter of time before the two of you will be—"

"Betrothed?" Mama suggested with a laugh. "I'd better head off to bed before I hear any more of your plan to marry off my youngest child. Good night Mother. Good night, Flora."

Flora bid the others good night and headed upstairs, plans for tomorrow forming in her mind to distract her from the troubling thoughts of Mama's and Grandma's teasing. There was the Lindberg broom to be replaced, two dogs to find for Mr. Brinks, and Big Boy still needed a permanent home. But as sleep grew nearer, questions about Sven dogged her. When she arose, the same worrisome thoughts that had ushered her into dreamland were on her mind.

CHAPTER 12

After the dogs' morning needs had been met, Flora set out for the Company Store. There, she dutifully, but reluctantly parted with half of the fifty cents she had earned from garden produce to purchase the new broom. When she had delivered it to her neighbor, she made a trip up Furnace Hill to weed and water the garden. She was on her way home intending to get an early start on her baking when she noticed two chesty male dogs tussling in the street outside the stock barn. She stepped inside to ask Mr. Ferris, the barn boss, who owned the white dogs with the brown markings.

He shooed a fly away with his hat. "Don't know who owns them. Don't believe I ever saw 'em before today. They're nothing but a nuisance, far as I can tell. Had to chase 'em out of here with a pitch fork not ten minutes ago."

When she had inquired further as to the ownership of the mutts and found no one, she went to the Company Store to purchase a wedge of cheese that she had Mr.

Powell cut into small cubes. Then she returned to Mr. Ferris.

"If you'll loan me two lengths of rope, I'll get those dogs out of your way and return the ropes to you promptly."

"Be glad to."

With the cheese as bait, she soon had the dogs leashed and walking eagerly beside her. At home, she tied them on opposite sides of the back yard with her own ropes, despite protests from Pet and Big Boy. She went inside and explained about the dogs to Mama and Grandma, warning them to keep their distance. Then she returned Mr. Ferris's ropes and left word at the Company Store for Frank Brinks to come see her the next time he was in town. She had started for home when she heard someone call her name. George Harris was beckoning to her from the door of his shop. He greeted her with furrowed brows.

"Someone broke in here again last night. Nearly sawed the lock off my meat locker. Something must have scared them off because they didn't get into the locker, and nothing's missing. But I don't want to take any more chances. Bring me that big mutt of yours at closing time. I'll try him out and see if he earns his keep."

"I'll have him here just before five." Flora's spirits lifted. Big Boy would have a new home. She'd miss him, but she could see him anytime at the meat market.

She had nearly reached home when the rattle of a wagon on the road behind her made her step off to the side. The unmistakably gruff voice of Frank Brinks greeted her.

"Miss McAdams, I heard you've got some dogs for me."

"They're tied in my back yard. I'll show you."

He parked in front and followed her. The moment he stepped into the back yard, all four dogs began barking. As he neared one of the bulldog-like males, the dog bared his teeth and growled.

Brinks ignored the warning, moving closer. The moment he came within reach, the dog latched onto the cuff of Brinks' pants and thrashed violently, tearing off a swatch before the man could back away.

Brinks let out a contemptuous laugh. "You're just what I'm looking for." With a gaze at the other similar dog, he added, "That one, too. Good job, Miss McAdams. Here's a little something for your trouble." He dropped a handful of change into her palm. "Now, to get 'em onto my wagon."

"I'll do it, Mr. Brinks. I'm going inside to get some cheese. Why don't you wait in your wagon?"

Reluctantly, he did as she suggested.

Flora headed for the house and then turned back. "Are you sure you want them, Mr. Brinks? I'm afraid they'll tear you apart once you get them home."

"Not a chance."

A couple of minutes later Flora loaded the dogs onto the bed of Brinks' wagon, tied them securely, then watched with mixed feelings as he drove away. She didn't know why she should be bothered by the prospect of turning two cantankerous strays over to an even more cantankerous owner.

Pushing the thought from her mind, she went inside to deal with a much sweeter prospect—baking taffy tarts. She prayed that her work in the kitchen and Mama's skill with a needle would yield results pleasing to Sven. Butterflies stirred in her stomach at the possibility that he might be more interested in *her* than in the tarts or his shirt.

~~~

Sven's day at the Machine Shop progressed as usual to the sound of the steam engine chugging and hissing its regular rhythm. He thought of it as the heartbeat of the furnace operation, keeping all the machinery and the engine of the charcoal train in proper running order. But today, another thought played counter rhythm in his mind. This evening, he would visit Miss Flora McAdams to claim his shirt and his tart. The prospect replaced the slow, strong beat inside his chest with the rapid, erratic pitter-patter of a telegrapher sending a message.

He shoved thoughts of Flora aside to concentrate on the task at hand; fashioning a connecting rod for the charcoal train. This, and a series of varied tasks filled his day, a day that seemed too long for the anticipation of his evening plans. But somehow, between thoughts of Flora and repairs to machines, tools, and the charcoal train engine, he had made it to the last hour and the last chore of the afternoon— drilling small, precise holes in a piece of sheet metal that was to replace a broken shroud. He was on the last hole when the belt flew off the steam engine, grazed the top of his head, and crashed into the window shattering two panes of glass, and any hopes of completing the repairs in time to visit Miss McAdams after supper.

CHAPTER 13

At half-past four in the afternoon, beneath gathering clouds and a freshening wind that smelled like rain, Flora tied a leash to Big Boy's collar and headed for Harris's. Grappling with mixed emotions, she told herself she must make this parting as quick as possible, not only for her own sake, but for Big Boy's. And for the sake of the taffy tarts waiting to be sold at the five o'clock whistle.

The day had been a productive one in the kitchen, baking taffy tarts not only for the family, but also to earn money for animal welfare. Thankfully, Mr. Brinks' coins had covered the money spent on Mrs. Lindberg's broom and on the cheese purchased to lure the dogs onto the bed of the man's wagon, but more supplies would soon be needed.

At the distant sound of thunder, she glanced skyward and whispered a prayer that the rain would hold off long enough to sell tarts. Approaching Harris's, she glanced across the way at the Machine Shop. Four panes of glass were missing from the front window and lay shattered in a heap on the ground. What had happened?

She knocked on Harris's back door and the moment he opened it, she asked about the Machine Shop window.

"Happened about a half hour ago. The main belt broke and flew off the steam engine straight through the window. It's a wonder neither Louis nor that new fellow were hurt. Wouldn't want to be them, though, working through the night to make repairs."

Obviously, Sven would not be coming to fetch his shirt or his taffy tart this evening. Thunder rumbled again, a little closer this time. She handed George the rope leash. "Here's Big Boy. He ought to do a fine job for you. Be sure to give him regular food and water."

George reached for the leash and Big Boy licked his hand. "Now, what kind of a guard dog will you make, slobbering all over me like I was your long lost friend?"

Flora laughed. "He's just getting a taste of the beef you've been butchering. He'll scare intruders away. Guaranteed!" Swiftly, she turned for home to fetch her tray of tarts, telling Mama and Grandma about the broken belt and window at the Machine Shop, adding, "Mr. Jorgensen won't be coming tonight, I'm sure."

"Why not go to the Machine Shop first thing? Mama asked. "Leave Mr. Jorgensen and Mr. Follo some taffy tarts to take the edge off their appetites while they're working late."

"That's a fine idea," Grandma said. "And don't charge for them."

Flora opened her mouth, ready to protest giving away the very pastries she intended for profit.

Grandma continued. "It's probably going to rain before you can sell the tarts anyway, and you can't sell them tomorrow because they won't be fresh. So you might as well give a few away."

Mama offered Flora a piece of oilcloth. "If the rain starts, you can keep your taffy tarts dry with this."

Flora tucked the oilcloth beneath her arm and set out for town with a full tray of tarts and a collection jar. She was only halfway to the furnace when sprinkles began to fall. She covered the tarts and continued as far as the Machine Shop. Inside, Louis Follo, a few years older and several pounds heavier than Sven, was busy putting a new belt on the steam engine while Sven tended to replacement of the broken windowpanes. Neither took notice of her standing in the doorway until she announced her presence.

"Come and get your fresh taffy tarts. On the house tonight!"

Both men looked up with a smile. Wiping their hands on rags that looked too oily to do much good, they helped themselves to a tart apiece and instantly consumed them with words of praise and thanks.

"You're welcome," Flora replied. "Sorry about your broken belt and window. I know you fellows will be working late tonight. I'll leave a few tarts to tide you over till you get home to supper." She pulled a clean handkerchief from her pocket, spread it on a stool, and set out a half dozen tarts, receiving more expressions of gratefulness.

When Louis had returned to his work, Sven said quietly, "About tonight—"

"I know you're tied up here. Come tomorrow night, if that's all right. Your shirt and taffy tart are waiting for you."

"Tart? But . . ." He indicated the tarts she had left on the stool.

"Like I said, those are on the house. I still owe you the taffy tart you paid for last week."

He grinned. "Tomorrow night."

Flora turned to go, covering her remaining tarts carefully with the oilcloth and stepping out into weather that had turned from sprinkles to drizzle. The five o'clock whistle blew, then a flash of lightning and crack of thunder sped her pace toward home.

By the time supper was over, the rain had passed. She fed Pet and took him for a walk down Stewart Avenue then up Sheldon, pleased with the way the dog had learned to move on three legs almost as well as on four. Flora was whispering a prayer of thanks for Pet's good health, good nature, and obedient manner when someone called her name. She turned to find Mrs. Follo standing in her open doorway.

"Miss McAdams, have you seen any sign of my husband? I expected him home for supper an hour ago."

"Good glory! Didn't you hear about the accident?"

"Accident? What accident? Is my husband—"

"He's fine." Flora approached her to explain about the broken belt and window, and the taffy tarts she had left for the men.

Looking pale and tired, and seemingly overcome with relief, Mrs. Follo lowered herself to sit on the threshold. "Bless you, Miss McAdams. I truly appreciate your thoughtfulness." One hand on her forehead, and the other resting on her belly, she said, "I've been feeling poorly today—I'm in the family way—haven't had much appetite. I did manage to cook up some supper for Louis. But when he didn't come home, I began to worry. I felt too queasy to go down and look for him. His meal is in the warming oven. It'll still be here waiting for him when he finally gets finished at the shop. Did he say when that will be?"

Flora shook her head. "Sorry. He didn't say." She thought a moment, an idea coming to her. "Mrs. Follo, if you'd like, I'll carry supper down to Mr. Follo for you."

Her countenance brightened. "Would you, really? I hate to inconvenience you."

"Good glory, it's no trouble! I'll take Pet home, and be back in a few minutes."

"Thank you, Miss McAdams. Thank you!"

Flora hurried off, her thoughts racing ahead of her. Was Mrs. Lindberg was still holding Sven's supper in the warming oven? If not, Mama would make up a plate for him and help her carry it down to the Machine Shop. Minutes later, the plan was in action, Flora carrying supper for Sven, Mama carrying the meal meant for Mr. Follo.

Approaching the Machine Shop, Flora saw that the broken windowpanes had already been cleaned up and replaced. When she and Mama stepped through the door, both men were hard at work on the steam engine, unaware of their visitors. Flora glanced at the stool where she had left her handkerchief and half-a-dozen tarts earlier. It was completely bare.

Mama announced their arrival. "Good evening, gentlemen. Hot supper has arrived. Can you spare a few minutes to take nourishment?"

With words of thanks, they redirected their focus from the steam engine repair to the plates of hot food Flora and Mama set before them. Flora explained to Mr. Follo that his wife, although unable to come herself, was resting quietly at home. Sven seemed to be listening carefully to her every word and watching closely her every move. She considered inquiring about her handkerchief, but decided to leave the question unasked. He would likely return it when he called for his shirt and tart.

Mama made small talk while the men ate, and in no time they had cleaned their plates and polished off the four taffy tarts offered for dessert. With more expressions of gratitude the men resumed their work and Flora and Mama started for home to wash and return dishes.

When Flora went to draw water at the well, she found Elin and her brother in conversation in the back yard with Pet snuggled between them soaking up affection. The vision returned to her later when she tucked herself into bed. She couldn't help replacing the couple in the picture with herself and Sven. But would she ever be able to engage the quiet Norwegian in a conversation of more than a few words, or understand what he was thinking and feeling? Maybe tomorrow, when Sven came for his shirt and tart . . . .

CHAPTER 14

At midnight, through gale force winds and driving rain, Sven returned to Mrs. Lindberg's and dropped into bed, exhausted from the long day's work. But he was not too tired to see the pretty face and taste the sweet taffy tarts of Miss Flora McAdams in his dreams. Morning arrived far too swiftly. Before he knew it, his fellow boarders were rousting him out of bed. Though badly fatigued, the thought of making his call at the McAdams home to claim his shirt and his tart put a spring in his step. As he made his way to the Machine Shop through a brisk breeze, huge waves rolled across the bay. He prayed that the steel due in for repair of the train's boiler would arrive soon enough to complete the job by quitting time.

Once the shop's steam engine was up and running, hissing and chugging in its usual fashion, Sven turned his back to Louis Follo and pulled Flora's handkerchief from his pocket. Holding it briefly to his nose, he took in the combined essences of taffy tart and lilac sachet, a scent as unique as its owner, then he tucked it away

again and resumed his work, wishing away the hours until the five o'clock whistle.

~~~

Flora's waking thought mirrored the last one before
she had fallen asleep. Today, Sven would call after supper for his shirt and tart. She pondered the pleasant
thought for a few moments and then threw off the covers.

Once breakfast was over, her busy day began with
Pet, walking and training him. Then she headed up Furnace Hill to do the weeding, watering, and harvesting at
the garden. Beans and pickles filled the baskets she
brought home, while thoughts of Sven filled her mind,
and continued to linger there during a return trip to the
garden with Mama to carry home the two watermelons
they would enjoy and use for pickling as well. While
Mama and Grandma washed the harvest in preparation
for preserving, Flora headed back down Stewart Avenue
in hopes of finding someone who would donate an object
that could be raffled off at the ball in order to earn money for animal welfare.

She stopped first at Harris's market, checking on Big
Boy who was tied outside the back door. He was over-
joyed to see her and at George's suggestion, she took
him for a walk. Her feet carried her on a route past the
open door of the Machine Shop where she caught a
glimpse of Sven, so hard at work that he did not even see
her pass by. She was sure that he hadn't wasted a mo-

ment's thought today on his promise to come this evening for his shirt and tart.

And I won't waste any time on it either, she silently promised herself. Directing her thoughts toward the raffle and her footsteps toward Harris's, she posed her request for a donation to George.

He scratched his chin. "Things are a bit tight right now. I'm trying to save up what little extra I earn to replace my stolen rifle before the Thanksgiving Day turkey shoot."

Mention of the Thanksgiving Day turkey shoot nearly launched Flora into a tirade on the cruelty of tying a turkey to a target for the purpose of shooting it, but she bit her tongue, allowing George to continue.

"The most I could give away would be a sirloin steak, and I don't think that would bring you much cash."

"Thanks anyway, George." Determined to find just the right item to bring good ticket sales, she headed for the Company Store. Mr. Powell offered a work shirt and pair of pants that hadn't sold yet on the clearance sale, and Henry Pinchin promised to give her one of his fancy pigeons when the eggs had hatched. Thanking them for their offers, she moved on, in search of a more substantial contribution. Mr. Ferris at the stock barn offered to part with a harness that had seen better days. Mr. Hines at the sawmill offered fifty board feet of 4" by 4" pine. Mr. Grennell, the master carpenter, offered a cigar humidor he had made with an image of the Fayette Furnace burned on the cover. Mr. Cumberland at the blacksmith shop was willing to donate a hammer. And Maggie Coughlin, the seamstress on Sheldon Avenue offered a stack of swatches that could be sewn into a crazy quilt. Disappointed, and out of ideas where to turn next, Flora headed home. When the family had gathered for the midday meal, she told of her unfruitful experience in town.

Papa offered a hopeful smile. "Something will come along."

"What about that abandoned old sleigh up on the bluff?" Toby asked. "If that were all fixed up, you could sell tickets in December and raffle it off just before Christmas."

Flora remembered the sleigh that had been sitting in the woods for at least ten years. "But who would fix it?"

Toby shrugged. "You've helped plenty of people in this town with hurting pets. Surely some of those folks ought to be willing to help you with the sleigh."

Mama's eyes lit. "I think the sleigh is a good idea, and ticket sales would be better in December anyway."

Grandma nodded. "The holidays always seem to put folks in a more generous frame of mind. Now, Flora, since we've all but solved your raffle problem, I hope you'll stay around here this afternoon. Your mother and I could sure use your help with the canning and pickling."

"Yes, Grandma." Her mind immediately strayed to finding someone willing and skilled enough to fix the old sleigh.

She continued to ponder the possibilities for the sleigh raffle throughout the afternoon—interspersed with di-vergent thoughts of Sven—while she washed the garden produce, cut up the watermelon rind for pickling, and assisted with the canning of the beans. With the amount of money a sleigh raffle would bring in, she could put up better kennels and improve the ones she already had.

Later, with canning and pickling chores over, she took fresh water to Pet and let him out of his kennel. He was especially glad to see her and she got the feeling maybe he was missing the company of Big Boy, as was she. Flora put Pet through his obedience commands and worked on teaching him how to play dead. He had nearly mastered the trick when Mama called her in to set the table.

She was just finishing the task as the five o'clock whistle sounded, causing her heart to stir. Sven would be heading home for supper and soon after that he would be here. She took a deep breath, returned to the kitchen to pour water into the glasses, and silently berated herself for the unsteadiness of her hands that slopped water all over the kitchen table.

Within minutes, the family gathered around the dining table, heads bowed while Papa asked the blessing.

"Almighty God, we thank Thee for the food set before us and ask Thy blessing upon it and each and every one at this table. In Jesus' name, Amen."

While he helped himself to the peas, potatoes, and ham balls, conversation turned to domestic topics, with Toby looking forward to the pickled watermelon Grandma had put up, and Mama mentioning the expected arrival of Mr. Jorgensen this evening to claim his shirt and taffy tart.

"I hope that means you'll invite the fellow in so we can all have the pleasure of his company," said Papa, "and of course some of Grandma's tea and Flora's taffy tarts."

Mama turned to Flora "If you will extend the invitation, perhaps Mr. Jorgensen will accept."

Flora's heart leapt to her throat. She hadn't counted on inviting Sven in, but rather had hoped for a more informal encounter in the back yard while she was tending to Pet. Thoughts of Sven in the parlor troubled her throughout the rest of the meal. She barely tasted the food in her mouth. When supper was over, she helped to clear the table, all the while wondering how long it would be until Sven came over. With a slightly shaky hand, she scraped leftovers into a bowl for Pet, eager to be outside with him. She headed for the back door but was only halfway across Grandma's room when Toby intercepted her.

"I'll take that out to Pet. Don't you have something else to do?" Forcing the bowl from her hand, he headed out back.

Flora began to follow until she saw Elin exiting her back door with a basin of dirty dish water for the garden behind the boardinghouse, and Toby offering to empty it for her. The favor earned him a beautiful smile and the opportunity for conversation. Although Flora wasn't privy to the words exchanged, she was fairly certain Elin was promising to see Toby when she finished her evening chores.

Upon her return to the kitchen, Flora offered to wash the dishes, but Mama sent her upstairs to freshen up. She checked first on Sven's shirt, finding it neatly folded on the hall table. The shoulder seam repaired by Mama looked no different than the seam on the other shoulder.

Carefully folding the shirt, she moved it to a table in the parlor across from the chair where Papa sat reading. For a moment, she simply stood in the middle of the room imagining Sven sitting at the end of the sofa. Her heart fluttered, sending her upstairs on winged feet to neaten her hair and wash her face with the specially scented lilac soap she had received for Christmas and that she had been using as a sachet for the handkerchiefs in her dresser drawer. When she had finished, she went down to take Pet out of his kennel for some exercise in the back yard. To her surprise, Toby already had the dog leashed and was headed for the road, Elin at his side.

Grandma called to Flora from the back stoop. "Please come in so I can take measurements for the dress you're going to wear to the ball."

How Flora detested dress fittings. She prayed that Sven would appear that very instant, but there was no sign of him. Reluctantly, she went inside.

Grandma held up the blue bodice of a dress Flora's older sister, Lavinia, had worn years ago. "Stand straight, shoulders erect, so I can see how this fits." She pressed the garment against Flora's back. "With a little letting out at the waist and a good, sturdy corset underneath to give you some shape, this will do just fine."

"Corset? I've no intention of stuffing myself into one of those torture garments just to wear a bodice that must be ten years old at the very least. Sorry, Grandma."

The old woman smiled. "No one will ever know how old it is when I'm finished. I'll turn this into a fashionable basque bodice with shirred panels down the front, and pleated, lacy cuffs on the sleeves. It will look just like the pictures in the new Butterick Pattern book." She pressed the catalog into Flora's hands.

Flora thumbed through the pages, and then Grandma held up a pink skirt that Mama had worn with a hoop many years ago. "You'll never recognize this old thing when I'm done making it narrower and adding drapes and gathers. Hold it up to your waist a minute and I'll check the length." She took the catalog from Flora's hands and set it aside to see where the hemline fell. "You're a little taller than your mother, but no matter. With all the ruffles and layers in vogue nowadays, I can make this skirt the right length. And of course, I'll add a train."

Flora opened her mouth to protest just as the knocker on the front door sounded.

Papa's voice carried all the way from the parlor. "Flora, would you answer that, please? And be sure to invite Mr. Jorgensen in."

Flora's heart raced as she hurried to do Papa's bidding.

CHAPTER 15

Flora had never seen Sven looking as neat as he did tonight with his hair all freshly combed and parted. She could even smell the essence of the bay rum hair oil he had used to bring order to his light brown curls. His shirt was fresh, neat, and crisp, showing his square shoulders and solid chest to good advantage. When he smiled, his eyes took on a hue as warm as the blue of Snail-Shell Harbor in summer.

He was the first to speak. "Good evening. I come for shirt and tart."

Though his words were brief, his voice carried a timbre that was music to Flora's ears. "Do come in, Mr. Jorgensen. Your shirt is ready and waiting for you in the parlor. You'll stay to tea, won't you?"

With a nod, Sven stepped inside and followed her.

In the parlor, Papa rose to greet him with a handshake while Flora made introductions. Then Mama appeared, introducing herself and directing Sven to a place on the sofa while she took the chair beside Papa.

When Sven had sat down, Flora fetched his shirt from the table and held it up for him to see. "I hope this will meet your approval. Thank you again for loaning your sleeve to a good cause. It certainly paid off for Pet."

She handed the shirt to him and perched on the opposite end of the couch, watching him closely as he looked over the repaired garment.

A pleased but puzzled look met Flora's gaze. "It is like new. No, better, done by an excellent seamstress." He folded it and laid it between them on the sofa.

Flora was about to credit Mama when she spoke up. "Flora comes from a long line of fine seamstresses. It seems to run in the family." She laughed at the unintended double meaning of her statement.

Flora was eager to make the truth known. "My mother is the one who—"

"Flora," Mama cut in, "please go and see if your grandmother needs help with the tea. And if Toby and Elin are out back, invite them to join us."

"Yes, Mama." When Flora found no sign of Toby, Elin, or Pet, she headed for the kitchen, catching a phrase here and there of the parlor conversation as she helped Grandma to finish setting the tray for tea and taffy tarts. How she longed to hear every word of response to Papa's inquiry about Sven's family in Norway, but his voice was too mellow to project beyond the parlor walls.

A couple of minutes later Flora carried the tea tray to the parlor for Grandma.

When the tea had been poured and the taffy tarts passed, Papa said, "Mr. Jorgensen was telling us a few minutes ago that he comes from a farming family in southern Norway near the Atlantic coast. He still has a mother, two younger sisters, and two younger brothers in the Old Country. They all attend the Lutheran Church."

"Don't you miss your family?" Grandma asked.

Sven nodded. "They send letters. Life there is hard. Here is much better."

"Mr. Jorgensen told us that he moved to Canada a few years ago," said Mama, "and met Louis Follo. Then Louis moved to Fayette. After Mr. Schiling's accident, Louis wrote and asked him to take the job here."

"Welcome, Mr. Jorgensen." Grandma offered a smile. "I surely hope you're settling in all right here, with your new job, and all."

Sven nodded. "It goes well for me . . . with possible exception of dogs." He grinned. "Too many!"

Papa chuckled. "You won't find an argument from anyone about that, least of all, Flora. She's constantly doctoring dogs that get into accidents and fights."

"And she tries to find homes for the strays." Mama stirred her tea. "Just yesterday she paired up two dogs with Mr. Brinks, although why he would want such nasty creatures as those is a puzzle to me."

"He probably wanted them to guard the tavern when he's not there," said Flora.

"Probably so." Grandma's gaze settled on Sven. "Seeing you're Norwegian, I imagine you have some good tales to tell about the trolls. And the Vikings—they believed in gods of this or that before Christianity came to your motherland, didn't they?"

Sven nodded. "We have many stories of trolls and Viking gods."

"What exactly is a troll, anyway?" Flora asked.

Sven laughed. "No two the same. They live in caves or hills. Some are giants. Some are dwarfs. Some have two heads. Some have one eye. One thing is same for all trolls. They hide from sun."

"Why is that?"

"In sun, they turn to stone."

Flora laughed. "Then there must have been a whole city of trolls here at Fayette a long time ago, judging from the limestone cliffs and the amount of rocks in the soil at the garden."

Sven smiled. "Maybe so."

In the lull that followed, Mama passed the tarts, encouraging everyone, especially Sven, to take seconds. Then she sat again and focused on Sven.

"Mr. Jorgensen, are you or any of the other fellows at Mrs. Lindberg's planning to attend the ball that's to be held on the third of October?"

Flora cringed. Where was Mama headed with that topic?

Sven shook his head. "No one plans to go."

"Would some of you go if you knew how to dance?"

The color rose in Sven's cheeks and invaded his forehead, causing the warmth in Flora's face to rise sharply. But changing the subject now would be too rude.

Sven shrugged. "Perhaps, if some knew how to dance, they would go to the ball."

"Then I will teach them." Mama smiled. "I'm sure some of my friends—all matronly ladies—would serve as dance partners, thus avoiding any reason for embarrassment. I'll inquire about holding the lessons at the town hall, then pass the word along to you fellows."

Flora was determined to change the subject. "Now that that's settled, I have a question for Papa and Mr. Jorgensen. I wondered if each of you would be willing to lend a hand, fixing that old pole cutter that's up on the bluff?" She referred to the abandoned sleigh that Toby had mentioned at the midday meal, explaining to Sven her idea to sell raffle tickets on it in December and hold the drawing just before Christmas. "I'm going to set up more kennels out back to hold the sick animals until they're well enough to release, and the stray dogs and cats until I find homes for them. I'm going to have a sort of animal clinic and shelter all in one. But I need money to pay for it."

Sven smiled. "Ambitious plans. My mother would say, 'Don't sell the pelts before you have shot the bear.' She was fond of that proverb."

"That's why I need help. *Your* help. And Papa's and Toby's and anybody else's who's willing."

"I'll help you, Flora." Papa took a sip of tea. "I'm sure Toby will, too."

Mama's gaze settled on Sven. "Flora has helped plenty of people in this town with their ailing pets. There ought to be quite a few who would lend a hand to fix the sleigh, like Henry Hines over at the sawmill." Mama turned to Flora. "Remember that time he brought his dog over here, full of porcupine quills, and you had to remove them?"

Flora nodded. "I pulled ten quills out of that creature's mouth."

"Maybe Mr. Hines would mill some lumber for the boards that need replacing in the sleigh," Papa suggested.

"I'll never forget that time Mr. Grennell's dog got sprayed by a skunk." Grandma's nose wrinkled. "What a stink that raised. He was so grateful when you got rid of the smell for him. He ought to be willing to turn that lumber you'll get from Mr. Hines into a new seat."

"And there's Mr. Cumberland over at the blacksmith shop," Papa recalled. "His dog had the worst sounding cough I ever heard when he brought him over here. Ten days later, he went home perfectly well. He might be willing to work on the runners."

Mama nodded. "And the upholstery will surely need replacing. Flora, remember when you healed Maggie Coughlin's kitten of tonsillitis a couple of years ago? She loves that cat dearly. I believe she'd do the upholstery, if you ask."

"And what about Mr. Young?" Grandma asked. "You fixed up his cat a few days ago. And not long ago you helped Henry Pinchin to make a decision about which type of fancy pigeons he should order from that breeder down in Illinois."

Flora nodded. "And I got rid of those nasty dogs that were troubling Mr. Ferris at the stock barn and took care of Mr. Powell's cat—the one he has in the warehouse over by the store—when she was lame. Maybe he'd donate upholstery fabric."

Sven's gaze settled on Flora. "Miss McAdams, your family has convinced me. I answer you now. Yes, I will help your father and brother with the sleigh."

A moment lapsed. Then Flora laughed, and her family too, over how carried away they had gotten from her original question. When the laughter died down, Flora's gaze met Sven's, held by the warmth of his blue eyes. "I thank you for your offer, Mr. Jorgensen. I'm grateful that you're willing to lend a hand."

Sven smiled.

In the distance a steamboat whistle sounded. Sven quickly checked his pocket watch. "Excuse, please. I go unload steel delayed by storm. We repair boiler for train now." He set his teacup on the tray and picked up his shirt.

Grandma was on her feet, tucking tarts into a napkin. "Take these along with you, Mr. Jorgensen."

Sven accepted Grandma's offer with a nod and a smile. His gaze took in her, Flora, and Mama. "Thank you for tea and tarts."

Mama smiled. "You're perfectly welcome, Mr. Jorgensen. Come again when you can stay longer."

Flora and Papa walked with Sven toward the door. "Do come again, son. Good night." Papa retreated to the parlor.

Flora gazed up into Sven's eyes. "Thank you for coming tonight, Mr. Jorgensen."

"Thank you for inviting me in." His quiet words carried a depth of meaning and his blue eyes grew earnest. "I like your family. And I look forward to working on your sleigh."

With that, he was gone, and to Flora's dismay, a piece of her heart went with him.

CHAPTER 16

Three weeks later
Wednesday, October 1

The morning sun shone through Flora's window, falling softly on her cheek and nudging her from a sound sleep. She sat up and propped herself against the extra pillows she'd been using since the onset of the flu that had knocked her off her feet with a fever, chest congestion, incessant coughing, and aches and pains that had penetrated every muscle of her body.

Gazing out the window, she thought back to the night when Sven had come for his shirt and tart. She could remember it as if it were yesterday, yet in a way it seemed as if it had never happened. In the days immediately afterward, she had been extremely busy. Harvesting vegetables, helping Mama and Grandma with canning and preserving, treating a dog for mange, assisting Dr. Bellows with his rare breeds of chickens, and helping Henry Pinchin with the new pair of fantail pigeons he had ordered from the breeder in Illinois had filled her days.

Lessons in the mazurka, two-step, gallop, and the Grand March that would open the ball had filled three of her evenings—lessons that included Toby and Elin even though she could not attend the ball. A baseball game and two horse races had occupied three of the other evenings, and she had even caught glimpses of Sven enjoying those events with his friends. Then, on the very day she and Dr. Bellows were to perform surgery to neuter Pet, illness set in and she lost contact with all but family, except for the good doctor's daily visits.

Day after day she barely managed to crawl out of bed for the necessities of life. Grandma sent up cups of chicken broth and bowls of crackers and cream. Mama made warmed milk sweetened by sugar and thickened by arrowroot, and the special recipe of milk toast that she always cooked for sick family members.

News of the outside world came piecemeal. Mama told her that Sven had stopped by to return the napkin Grandma had given him with the tarts, and had wished Flora a speedy recovery. Toby had told her that the abandoned sleigh had been moved to a shed where work could be done on it, thanks to Mr. Ferris, the barn boss, who had hitched up a couple of his best draft horses for the job. Papa had told her that Sven had taken ownership of the project, recruiting help from among those whose animals Flora had healed. And Mama had told her that under no circumstances was she to go looking for the sleigh once she was well enough to be out and about.

"Sven has made it clear that you are not to be allowed to see the sleigh or even know the exact location of its whereabouts until it is fully restored and ready to put on display to sell raffle tickets," Mama had stated in no uncertain terms. And for several days afterward, Flora had been too weak to give much thought to spying out the location where the sleigh might be hiding.

But those days were past. This morning, for the first time in two weeks, she didn't feel the urge to cough, or the grip of fatigue, or the aches and pains that had plagued her muscles. For the first time since her mama's stern warning, she was tempted to undertake a thorough search of every shed in the village to get a glimpse of the sleigh.

In a burst of enthusiasm, she threw off the covers and sprang to her feet, then immediately sat down on the edge of her bed. Her legs weren't quite as steady as she had expected. She rose more slowly and made her way to the wash stand, gaining strength and confidence that by day's end, she would be feeling like her old self again. And just in time, too, for today was the first day of October. Two nights from this evening, the ball would be held in the Town Hall, and she would not disappoint Big Toby by missing it for health reasons.

Flora opened her wardrobe and reached for the dress with the blue bodice and pink skirt that Grandma had made for the ball. When she held it up to herself in front of the mirror, she was surprised at the amount of weight she had lost during her illness. For the first time in her life, she actually had a waistline! Her shape fit perfectly that of the stylish boned bodice Grandma had so lovingly fashioned. Even Flora's face had gained a new shape with hollows in her cheeks where none had been before.

As she gazed at herself in the mirror, she couldn't help wondering if Sven would be at the ball. Mama had told her that her offer of dance lessons for the young men of the village had succeeded nicely, wisely scheduled for the evenings when there were no horse races or baseball games. Mama had confided, too, that Sven was one of her best pupils.

With a sigh, Flora put the gown away. Attending the ball with Sven was an impossible dream. But she hoped that he would put in an appearance and agree to fill one of the lines on her dance card.

Setting aside thoughts of the upcoming ball, she reached for her gray plaid skirt and pinstriped blouse waist, surprised at how loosely they now hung on her. And when she headed downstairs, she was surprised, too, at how much more slowly she needed to take the steps.

Grandma's hearty breakfast of fried eggs, bacon, and a slice of extra thick toast increased her strength and energy. Again she wondered where the sleigh was being kept. She carried her plate and silverware to the kitchen where Mama and Grandma were washing dishes.

"Mama, Grandma, I'm going to take Pet for a walk."

Mama regarded her with narrowed brows. "Are you sure you feel up to it?"

Grandma raised her finger. "You'd better not overdo, or you'll be right back in bed again."

"I'll go slow. And I'll come home as soon as I feel tired. I promise."

"And you'd better promise one thing more." Mama shook a spatula at her. "You'd better promise me that you aren't going to look for that sleigh. Mr. Jorgensen would be greatly disappointed if you spoiled his plan and saw it before it is finished."

How could Mama have read her mind? "I promise."

Flora put on her cloak and the straw hat with the notch in the brim and stepped out the back door, heading straight for Pet's kennel. She had seen him briefly on each of the last few days when her brother had brought him up to her room to visit. At the sight of her now, Pet's tail began to wag his whole body. He whimpered with glee and sat close to his kennel door, scratching it with his one front paw. She let him out and knelt to fasten his leash, receiving a face washing from his eager, wet tongue.

She laughed and hugged his wiggling body, the distinctive scent of his glistening coat filling her nostrils. "It seems you missed me as much as I missed you. Do you want to go for a walk?"

He barked, and much to her surprise, began to heal perfectly at her left side. Toby had been walking Pet nightly, often in the company of Elin, and had evidently been doing a good job of training in the process.

Down Stewart Avenue they went. Flora intended to call at Harris's to see how Big Boy was doing, then walk past the Machine Shop hoping to catch a glimpse of Sven. She had gone as far as the hotel when she heard Big Toby's voice.

"Miss Flora! Wait up!"

CHAPTER 17

Big Toby ran toward Flora from the back of the hotel. The moment he reached Pet, he went down on one knee. With pats and hugs and quiet words of praise he lavished affection on the three-legged pup who returned the favor with wide sweeps of his wagging tail and broad licks with his tongue against Big Toby's face and hands. When the two had finished their greeting, Big Toby rose to his feet, his blue eyes sparkling.

"Miss Flora, I'm glad to see you. I heard you were awfully sick."

"You heard right, but I'm well again now, and with a little review, I'll be all practiced up on my dance steps for the ball. Are you?"

"I . . . uh . . ." His face grew scarlet, then his words came in a rush. "Miss Flora, I can't take you to the ball. I hope you understand. It's not that I don't want to. I just can't. I didn't think you'd be able to go, being so sick and all, and this new girl came to the hotel to work last week. She's Mrs. Harris's niece. And she's kind of like me in the head, you know?"

Flora nodded.

"Anyway, she and I are best friends now, and when she heard about the ball she insisted that I take her. Then Mrs. Harris went all the way to Escanaba and bought her a special gown. It was real costly and it's real pretty and, well, Jane would just die of disappointment if she didn't wear it to the ball Friday night. You know what I mean?"

Flora put on a smile. "Big Toby, I understand completely. I hope you and your new friend have a wonderful time at the ball. In fact, I'm going to say a prayer for you and—Jane, is it?"

He nodded enthusiastically.

"I'm going to say a prayer for you and Jane and ask God to bless your new friendship and to help you to have a wonderful time at the ball."

"Thank you, Miss Flora. I gotta get back to work now." As quickly as he'd appeared, he disappeared around the back side of the hotel.

Flora turned to go. How wonderful for Big Toby to have a new friend. And now, it seemed that God had granted her wish not to attend the ball. Too bad Grandma's work on a gown and Mama's and Papa's lessons on dance steps would go to waste. At least the dance teachings had brought her brother and Elin together.

Flora continued on her way, heading toward the back of Harris's to check on Big Boy. There, she found him tied to the stair rail, hiding under the back steps. The moment he saw her, he came out from underneath, barking with excitement. Pet pulled on his leash, as eager to greet his old friend as was Flora. She hugged and patted

Big Boy and he licked her hand. Then he and Pet greeted one another with the usual sniffs of the face and tail.

George hurried out the back door, his stained apron flapping in the breeze. Big Boy cowered, crawling back underneath the steps with a pitiful whine. George sent a disdainful look in Big Boy's direction and then focused on Flora.

"Am I ever glad to see you! Heard you were sick."

She nodded. "I'm well again now, thank goodness."

"And just in time. I'm at wit's end with this guard dog you gave me. You've got to take him back."

"What happened? Didn't he keep the burglars out?"

"He kept them out, all right. But he chewed up nearly every piece of wood in my shop in the meanwhile—the corner of my display counter, the legs on my butcher table, even my door frames! He's got to go!" George untied the rope from the rail and handed it to Flora.

"I'm sorry he didn't work out for you, George. I guess he's not happy all alone here at night."

"You can say that again." Head shaking, he returned to his shop.

Flora coaxed Big Boy from beneath the steps and led the dogs away from Harris's, pausing to give Big Boy a big hug. "Don't you worry, fellow. You're coming home with us. But first, let's take a little walk."

At the sound of the word "walk," Big Boy immediately perked up, barking and spinning in circles with such exuberance that he almost knocked Pet off his feet. The way Big Boy acted, it were as if he hadn't been walked at all since she'd last seen him. She chose a route past the Machine Shop hoping to catch a glimpse of Sven.

She could see him inside, bent over some machinery, but he didn't look up. Pushing aside the temptation to search for the sleigh in the sheds near the sawmill, she turned and headed for the bluff trail, drawing a deep breath of the crisp fall air. Despite the smell of furnace smoke, the day held an appeal of its own with a sky so intensely blue it seemed like something from an artist's brush. Passing the vegetable garden, she noticed that foliage had lost its color and was going dormant since her last visit.

On the rise to the bluff trail she paused to offer more affection to Big Boy and Pet and then set out again. At an opening atop the bluff she sat on the same old stump where she had sat as a young child, and took in the view. It hadn't changed much over the years except to reveal more of the houses along Sheldon Avenue where trees had been removed and turned into charcoal for the furnace. A tug towing a barge full of iron ore entered the harbor and a schooner loaded with iron pigs set sail for Cleveland. Even so, an accumulation of iron pigs, some cast as far back as four years ago, nearly filled the dock warehouse.

Boards lay stacked near the sawmill, and an accumulation of empty barrels and kegs lay helter-skelter by the shoreline. But beyond the docks and the bustle of the industrial harbor lay the ruffled waters of Big Bay, tossing steel blue waves into foamy white caps. They reminded her of her own life this day—learning that she was no longer needed by Big Toby, and discovering that Big Boy was neither needed nor wanted by George. She wrapped her arms about him and pressed her cheek alongside his hairy face. Pet pushed in between with a little whine and she included him in the hug, too.

"All is well, fellows. All is well. Let's go home." They rose and started down the bluff, their route taking them in the direction of the Machine Shop.

~~~

When Sven turned off the planer and headed out the door to take in some sunshine on his morning break, he hadn't expected the brightness to come in the form it did. But there, off in the distance, was Miss Flora McAdams walking two dogs. His heart thumped faster. He'd prayed for her daily from the moment he'd heard about her illness. And he'd missed seeing her more than he wanted to admit. He reached into his pocket and pulled out the handkerchief that belonged to her. He'd been waiting for the right time to return it. And not wanting to give it back empty, he'd given thought to what trinket he could tuck inside. Certain that he'd come up with the best solution to both the timing and the trinket, he shoved the gift back into his pocket and stepped off briskly toward her.

CHAPTER 18

Sven's sturdy frame, carried by purposeful strides, moved closer to Flora. Her heartbeat quickened. The dogs grew protective, jerking at their leashes and barking a warning.

Sven slowed his steps, speaking to the dogs with a low, gentle greeting until they grew calm and quiet. When Sven's gaze met Flora's, the smile she offered was reflected back to her in equal measure.

"Good morning, Miss McAdams. You are well again?"

"I am, thank you. And you? You have managed to avoid this loathsome flu, I trust?"

"I am well. And I have something of yours." He pulled her handkerchief from his pocket and offered it to her.

Holding both leashes with one hand, she reached for it with the other, seeing and feeling that some small item was hidden inside the cotton square, but unable to unwrap it single-handed.

Sven reached for the leashes. "Open!"

Carefully, she unfolded the fabric to reveal a carved wooden character with hair of shaggy wool, a nose oversized for its face, a ragged woolen shirt, and patched leather knee pants. She offered Sven a quizzical look.

"Troll." Sven grinned. "From my sister. She gave it to me the day I left my country. Now, he is yours."

Flora held him up, turning him this way and that in the bright sun. "I see *this* troll hasn't turned to rock in the sunshine."

Sven laughed. "He is special case."

"He is, indeed. Thank you, Mr. Jorgensen. And I shall find a special place for him when I get home."

With a nod, he handed the leashes to her, bid her good day, and headed back to the Machine Shop.

Flora pressed the handkerchief and troll into her pocket and continued toward home. What was the implication of this unusual gift? No matter. She would treasure it as one of her most cherished possessions.

She hadn't gone far when she heard the rattle of a wagon behind her. As she stepped off the road, the gravelly voice of Frank Brinks greeted her.

"Miss McAdams, those two mutts you got for me are fine, scrappy fellows. You wouldn't have another pair like 'em, would you?"

She gazed up into his disfigured face and shook her head. "Sorry, Mr. Brinks."

"If you come across some, let me know. I'll make it worth your trouble, a dollar apiece." With a shout to his team and a crack of his whip, he was gone.

The prospect of acquiring two dollars for more kennels and supplies held great appeal, but Flora pushed the idea from her mind, certain that there was no possibility of finding two stray dogs as cantankerous as the pair she had already given Brinks.

Home again, she reassigned Big Boy to his former kennel, fed both dogs, and offered them fresh water, then went inside. When she had hung her cloak in the front hall she went to the kitchen and explained to Mama and Grandma why she would not be attending the ball with Big Toby.

"I'm so sorry, Grandma, about all the trouble you went to, making a dress for me. I'm afraid I won't get to wear it after all."

Grandma offered an understanding smile. "That's all right, child. Another opportunity will come along." She raised a crooked finger. "In my lifetime I've learned that when the Lord closes one door, He soon opens another."

Mama tucked an unruly strand of gray hair in amongst the darker ones. "Maybe you could convince your brother to take you."

Flora heaved a tired sigh. "I don't think he'd have any fun going with his little sister. If you'll excuse me, I think I'll get a little rest." She'd started for the stairs.

Mama's voice called after her. "Flora, I see you've brought Big Boy home again. Doesn't George need him?"

Flora returned to the kitchen. "Perhaps tomorrow I'll find someone else to take him. I'm too tired to think about it today."

In her room, Flora took out the tiny little troll and studied it again, then found a secret place for it beneath the lid of her trunk. Then she lay down on her bed for a nap.

~~~

With the evening meal over and the kitchen work finished, Flora set out with Pet and Big Boy for a walk down Stewart Avenue, thankful that her energy had returned somewhat following a second nap in the afternoon and a hearty supper of beef stew. She had decided to forego the contest between Jo Harris's trotter, Berry, and J.B. Kitchen's horse, Dick, at the racetrack. Papa, Toby, and most of the village were there now, leaving the town quieter than usual. Returning by way of Sheldon Avenue, she put Big Boy in his kennel and spent some time with Pet, reviewing the tricks she had taught him using cheese cubes as rewards.

Then, she began working with Big Boy. He had mastered the command for "sit" when Sven approached, breaking the dog's concentration and sending him into a fit of barking. Flora spoke to Big Boy reassuringly, luring him toward his kennel with a cheese cube, all the while wondering why Sven was here rather than at the races. Flora latched the kennel gate and turned to her visitor, searching out his blue eyes shaded by a brown plush hat.

Sven offered a nervous smile, and his Adam's apple bobbed. Why was he so tense?

Finally, he began to speak, each word carefully formed. "I talk to your father at race track. He permits me ask. May I have honor of escorting you to the ball?"

Stunned momentarily, Flora's answer burst forth. "Yes! Oh, yes! I will be *happy* to go to the ball with you!"

From his vest pocket he produced a dance card, opened it, and pointed to his initials penned in for the first dance, the Grand March, and the last dance, a waltz. He handed it to her. "I come Friday, nine o'clock. Yes?" His brow rose.

"Nine o'clock. I'll be ready."

With a nod, he turned and hurried off.

Flora glanced down at the card with its fancy border and the word "Programme" spelled out in large, decorative letters across the cover. She hugged it to her, then danced a little jig and flew to the house on winged feet to share her news with Mama and Grandma, who were busy fashioning elegant pine bough swag decorations for the big event.

CHAPTER 19

Two nights later, with gale force winds continuing their daylong blow outside, children's laughter and happy squeals spilled from the parlor, interspersed with their Uncle Toby's command to "catch whom you may" in a rollicking game of Blind-Man's Buff. Flora's sister and brother-in-law, Huck, and their three children—Violet, age eight; Dan, age six; and Rose, age four, had arrived from Sac Bay, six miles south of Fayette, in time for supper. The joyful voices were music to Flora's ears while she and her older sister, Lavinia, helped Mama and Grandma put the kitchen in order.

Later, with Toby and Grandma watching over the children, Lavinia and Huck would attend the ball with Mama and Papa. Flora reached for a clean plate and began to dry it, thankful that the dishes were almost done, and thankful, too, that her strength had improved sharply in the past two days. She would have plenty of energy for the evening's events, and could hardly wait for Sven to call for her.

But that was two hours away, and Flora had yet to bathe, fix her hair, and put on the gown Grandma had sewn for her. She was setting the clean plate in the cupboard when a loud, rapid knock sounded at the back door. She hurried through Grandma's room to answer.

Mrs. Lindberg stood on the back stoop, wind flapping at her apron and whipping at the strands of blonde hair that had come lose from her braid. "Good evening, Flora. May I speak with your brother please?" Though her request bore some urgency, she followed it with a tentative smile.

"Certainly, Mrs. Lindberg. Come in, won't you?" Flora shut the door on the cold wind and hurried to the parlor to summon Toby.

Leaving Huck and Papa in charge of the children, Toby sped to the back of the house.

All kitchen work ceased while Flora, along with Lavinia, Mama, and Grandma gathered near the door to Grandma's room to listen to Mrs. Lindberg's words.

"I am late to ask—perhaps too late. But ask I will. Please, take Elin to the ball tonight. She refused you earlier because our kinfolk from Sweden—cousins she has not seen in ten years—were to arrive today. But rough weather delayed them. She is free to go with you. Please?"

"I . . . I would like to take Elin to the ball, Mrs. Lindberg, truly, I would. But I'm to help Grandma look after my nieces and nephew tonight."

Grandma marched into the room, followed by Flora, Mama, and Lavinia.

Grandma's gaze pinned Toby. "Young man, I am perfectly capable of caring for Lavinia's brood without your help." She wagged her crooked finger at him.

Toby's cheeks colored deeply. "I—"

Mama interrupted. "Your grandmother is right, Toby. You *must* take Elin to the ball. After all, the two of you have practiced your dance steps until you could do them blindfolded."

Lavinia chimed in. "Besides, I'm planning to put the children down before Huck and I leave. Grandma will have three sleeping babes to care for."

Flora spoke up. "Elin will be mighty hurt if you pass up an evening at the ball with her to stay home with your nieces and nephew. I doubt she'll ever speak to you again if you don't take her dancing tonight."

Toby raised his hands in defeat and laughed. "Grandma, Mama, sisters, you're preaching to the converted." He turned to Mrs. Lindberg. "There's nothing I'd like more than to take your daughter to the ball tonight. Please tell Elin I'll come by at nine."

Mrs. Lindberg smiled. "I'll tell her. Thank you!"

When she had gone, Grandma told Toby, "Go and fetch your good shirt and necktie. I'll see that they're pressed while you wash up."

Toby bent to hug Grandma. "Thank you."

Grandma returned the hug and gave him a nudge. "Go on, now. Time's a-wasting!"

"Yes, ma'am." He sprinted for the stairs.

A minute later, Flora and her sister went into Mama and Papa's bedroom just off the kitchen where a tub had been filled with hot bath water for their baths. When they had finished they went up to the bedroom they had once shared to fix their hair and get dressed. Lavinia brushed Flora's hair softly back from her face, adding a coiled hairpiece to her own brown twist. Then, with patience and skill, Lavinia framed Flora's face with tiny little curls, giving her a sweet, almost angelic appearance.

Lavinia reached for the gown Grandma had made over for the occasion and helped Flora put it on, keeping her back to the mirror as she closed the eighteen buttons down the back. "I am amazed at how beautifully Grandma transformed my old dress. You will be right in style with the close-fitting bodice, shirred front panels, and long narrow sleeves with lacy cuffs."

Lavinia added a lacy jabot beneath Flora's chin. "There. The waist up looks wonderful. Now let me help you with the skirt." As Lavinia fussed with the drapes and folds and the knife-pleated train, Flora could hardly wait for a glimpse in the mirror.

Moments later, she turned to look at herself, unable to believe the picture of elegance that stared back at her. It was as if she were looking at someone she'd never seen before, so dramatic was the change.

Lavinia looked on, smiling. "What do you think, Flora?"

"I. . . I'm speechless!"

"Do you think your Mr. Jorgensen will approve?"

Flora's brows creased. "Good glory! I think Mr. Jorgensen will not even recognize me!"

Lavinia laughed. "I'll vouch for your true identity. Now help me with my hair and gown."

Flora, feeling somewhat inept, managed to fasten a chignon to her sister's shiny, dark brown hair with good results. Then she helped Lavinia don a blue-gray velvet-and-satin gown designed with an "armored effect" of alternating fabrics that ran in vertical panels down the bodice. The skirt bore a remarkable resemblance to Flora's in its design, with drapes and train, and when all of the buttons had been fastened, the skirt tapes tied, and a pewter brooch from Grandma pinned to a lacy jabot, Lavinia bore the look of faultless refinement in fashion.

She gazed at her image in the mirror, then pulled Flora into the picture. "Aren't we a pair of stylish sisters? The belles of the ball, I predict. Now, it's almost nine." She handed Flora a pair of white gloves. "Put these on. Then we'd better go downstairs."

While Lavinia rounded up her children and helped them put on their nightclothes, Flora drew profuse compliments from all but Grandma, who simply gazed at her, eyes glistening. Flora wrapped her arms about Grandma and spoke softly in her ear.

"Thank you, Grandma. I love you."

Grandma replied with a tight squeeze, then pulled a handkerchief from her pocket and dabbed away her happy tears.

Toby, looking spiffier than Flora had ever seen him in a crisply pressed white shirt, black silk bow tie, and smart jacket with wide lapels, pulled his watch from his vest pocket. "It's time for me to go. See you at the Town Hall." No sooner had he started for the door, than the knocker sounded.

Toby turned to Flora. "You'd better answer."

Heart fluttering, she stepped forward, praying that the evening to come would be as beautiful as her family had made her feel.

CHAPTER 20

Sven held the bouquet of tissue-wrapped zinnias close, shielding them from the fierce breeze, and silently prayed that his heart would stop mimicking the door-knocker he had just sounded. Taking a deep breath, he had begun to exhale when the door opened and the vision of beauty that smiled up at him literally snatched the wind from his lungs.

Unable to speak, he managed a feeble smile in return, struggling to reconcile the figure of grace and loveliness in the doorway with the less sophisticated image of Miss Flora McAdams that he carried in his mind. Stepping back, he gazed to his left and to his right to reassure himself that his nerves hadn't carried him past the girl's home. Then the sound of her voice removed any doubt.

"Good glory, Mr. Jorgensen! Where are you going?"

Sven offered a nervous laugh and stepped inside. "I bring flowers." He pressed them toward her, his gaze caught in the warmth of the brown eyes that looked up at him.

~~~

Flora had never seen Sven looking finer. His wonderfully wavy hair was still in place despite the wind, and his herringbone jacket and vest made the most of his lean, yet powerful form. But they couldn't hide the shakiness of his flower-laden hand, or the arresting blue of his eyes that revealed sentiments unspoken.

Flora took the flowers from Sven and peeled away the tissue to study the brilliant orange, yellow, and red of the bouquet—her first ever. Turning it this way and that, she spoke in hushed tones. "Thank you, Mr. Jorgensen. Your flowers are just beautiful!"

"You deserve better. Roses. But they are gone. Only zinnias left."

She gazed up into eyes. "Zinnias are perfect for me." She spared one last adoring glance at the flowers and then asked Grandma to put them in water.

With Sven's help, she donned her cloak and stepped out into a ferocious wind that whipped at the hem and tugged at the hood. Sven's arm went tightly about her, shielding her from the strong gusts and guiding her down Stewart Avenue.

To Flora's delight, the entire neighborhood, it seemed, was turning out for the ball—Dr. and Mrs. Bellows, Mr. and Mrs. Follo, Mr. and Mrs. Pinchin, Mr. and Mrs. Powell, and Henry Pinchin with Mary Caffey. Near the Town Hall, a row of carriages had already been parked, several others were pulling close, and a half-dozen couples were making their way on foot from the hotel across the street. Among those from the hotel were Big Toby and Jane, George Harris and his wife, Clara, and the master carpenter, Mr. Grennell with Harriet Harris's maid, Marian Phillips.

Folks from other parts of the town joined the throng—Joseph Marew with Maggie Coughlin and Charles Mason with Lillian Ruggles among them.

Such a crowd caused a slight crush in entering the hall. Sven drew her closer until they were safely inside where the elder Mrs. Harris greeted them and directed them to the separate areas that had been designated to serve as the ladies' and gentlemen's cloak rooms.

By the time Flora's cloak had been checked, Mama, Lavinia, and Elin had arrived. With great anticipation they helped one another restore hair and gowns to perfect order, then emerged to be led into the ballroom by their escorts.

Mrs. J.B. Kitchen, in a gown of forest green satin, welcomed them cordially while a small orchestra played softly. While waiting for the Grand March to open the ball, Flora gazed about the room, unable to recognize the plain wooden walls and ceiling that she had known.

From a huge silver globe hanging at the center of the hall, crepe streamers radiated outward to create a false ceiling. Their graceful drapes were caught up by ribbon flowers and bows fastened to freshly whitewashed walls. Pine bough swags, the very ones she had seen Mama and Grandma creating at home, hung a safe distance from the wall lanterns turned low.

Near one side of the hall stood a divider to set apart the refreshment area. There, several chairs had been placed near a table laden with delightful confections that included frosted grapes, plates of chocolate kisses, coconut cakes, lemon biscuits, miniature plum cakes, and brown sugar wafers. Frosted gourds stood amidst tea lights, and tall, tapered candles. And two giant crystal punch bowls encircled by matching cups held a tea-like beverage afloat with fruit slices and ice chips.

The ballroom was a quiet buzz of happy voices of guests seeking partners for the dances on the program. Since Sven would be Flora's partner for only the Grand March and for the last dance, a waltz, they both would need other partners for the dances in between. She was beginning to wonder who those other partners would be when Big Toby, with his friend Jane on his arm, approached.

"Miss Flora, you're so fancied up, I almost didn't know ya." His blue eyes sparkled. He nudged his friend forward. "This here is Miss Jane Bigelow, the new friend I told ya about. I told Jane all about *you,* too. Isn't she just the prettiest thing ya ever did see?"

"She is!" Flora admired the young woman's sweet smile, meticulously coifed honey-gold hair, and burgundy satin gown that flattered her trim figure.

When Flora had introduced the couple to Sven, Big Toby told her, "I came to ask if you'd honor me with your hand for the first waltz. Will ya?"

Checking the program, Flora saw that the first waltz followed the Grand March. "I'd love to."

Sven immediately invited Jane to be his partner for the same waltz, then she and Big Toby went in search of other partners.

No sooner had they stepped away than Charles Mason and Lillian Ruggles drew near. They seemed the perfect couple, both of them being of a tall, slender build, with Charles's dark hair and mustache making Lillian's blond hair seem even lighter than before.

When they had been introduced to Sven, Charles told Flora, "I came to ask for the honor of your hand for a dance tonight."

"Certainly." Flora offered her card and he placed his initials on a line for a gallop.

When Sven asked Lillian to be his partner for the same dance, Flora couldn't ignore the jealousy niggling within. She quickly pushed the feeling aside, moving about the floor with Sven to find partners for the other dances. Joseph Marew agreed to be her partner for a polka, and Henry Pinchin for a mazurka, but upon approaching each of them it seemed as if they didn't know Flora until they heard her voice.

She pondered that curious experience while enlisting Papa, Toby, Dr. Bellows, and her brother-in-law Huck as partners for other dances. By the time the Master of Ceremonies called for the Grand March to begin, Flora and Sven had found partners for most of the dances on the program.

CHAPTER 21

Stately music filled the air and couples formed—gentleman on the left, lady on the right—falling in behind Mr. and Mrs. J.B. Kitchen who led the Grand Promenade around the room to the end of the hall. Flora and Sven followed behind Big Toby and Jane, and were in turn followed by Charles Mason and Lillian Ruggles.

At the caller's direction, the Promenade turned and proceeded straight up the center of the room to the opposite end. Then the couples began casting off twos—one couple turning left and the next couple turning right until the whole company was divided in half and proceeding along the perimeters of the hall to the end. When the first two couples met at the center of the room, they formed a column of four and began the procedure all over again. Flora and Sven combined with Charles and Lillian in their group of four.

Upon reaching the other end of the hall, the groups of four dissolved into a single file that moved to the opposite end of the room then began weaving back and forth like a snake. At the end of the room once more, Mr. and Mrs. Kitchen faced each other and lifted their arms to form an arbor. In turn, each couple passed beneath the arbor, stepped back, and lifted their arms to extend the arbor until all the couples had passed through. The process delighted Flora who had participated in a limited version of the event in her parents' parlor during dance lessons. Now, taking part in an arbor of Town Hall proportions seemed fairytale-like, and she was tempted to pinch herself to make sure she wasn't dreaming. Surely Cinderella's ball was no grander than this.

Flora's thoughts quickly returned to the present as the last couple passed through the arches formed by Mr. and Mrs. Kitchen, who followed behind and in turn were being followed by the others who had made arches. Soon, Flora and Sven made their way through the remainder of the arbor and continued to follow the column of twos around the room one last time, coming to a halt when the music ended. Flora turned to Sven for the closing curtsey.

As she smiled up at him, he squeezed her hand, then let go. How she wished the next dance, and the one after that and the one after that could be with him. But social custom dictated otherwise. As the introduction to the waltz began, she turned to Big Toby and curtsied as Sven bowed to Miss Jane Bigelow.

As Big Toby's arm came firmly around Flora's waist and he took her hand in his, she sensed his confidence. With grace and accuracy he led her through the six-step pattern that she had practiced so diligently at home with Papa and Toby. Amidst the steps and turns, Flora caught sight of Toby on the other side of the room, paired up with Lillian Ruggles, while Elin danced in the arms of Charles Mason. Of the two couples, Charles and Elin seemed more comfortable together.

Not far from Flora, Sven and Jane were making their way around the room, although a tad stiffly. Flora offered a silent prayer of thanks that her dance with Big Toby was coming off so well. The melody of Strauss's *Tales from the Vienna Woods* lifted her spirits to a place above the silver globe that hung overhead, giving the impression that her feet were no longer flitting across the floor, but floating from cloud to cottony cloud in a celestial castle. When the final strain of the waltz had played out and the closing bow and curtsey had been given, Flora's feet touched down and Toby escorted her to a chair beside the refreshment table. She took a deep breath, preparing for the swift step-slide repetition of the gallop, the dance she had promised to Charles Mason.

He approached, offering her a cup of punch from the nearby crystal bowl and making conversation during the pause between dances. "Pleasant music, and tasty punch, don't you agree, Miss McAdams?"

Flora sipped the beverage. It tasted like an exceptionally sweet, fruity variation of iced tea. "Delicious punch. Thank you." She took another swallow. The combination of honey, lemon, orange, and lime was sliding past her tongue when a disturbance near the front door caught her attention.

Frank Brinks staggered into the hall, voice loud, words slurred. "So *thisss* is where everybody's gone to tonight!"

Guests stepped out of the way as the hefty man headed in the direction of the refreshment table. Coming to a halt near Flora, he reached for a cup of punch, spilling half of it down his filthy jacket and then raising the cup to his mouth. With a loud slurp, he tasted the beverage, then set the cup down with a thud that sloshed punch onto the white tablecloth leaving a large brown stain.

"Something's missin' from this punch," he drawled. "It ain't got no punch, know what I mean? You fellas need to come out to my place and get some *real* punch!" He laughed derisively.

The orchestra began to play the introduction to the gallop. Flora was thankful to exit the refreshment area and curtsey to Charles. But as he took her in his embrace, a powerful grip on her arm yanked her away.

Brinks pulled Flora to him, stepping on her train and ripping it. "This is *our* dance, ain't it, Miss McAdams?" His breath, hot in her face, stank of liquor and cigar smoke.

"Good glory! No!" Flora twisted away, but couldn't break free.

Charles moved in. "Leave the lady alone!" He shoved Brinks hard on the shoulder.

Brinks staggered back, taking Flora with him. Suddenly releasing her, he regained his equilibrium and headed toward Charles. "I'll teach *you* a lesson, *teacher!*"

CHAPTER 22

Like a freight train gaining steam, Brinks advanced toward Charles, rammed his shoulder into Charles's midsection, and backed him clear through the divider and into the refreshment table.

Crystal cups crashed to the floor. A tidal wave of punch overflowed the bowl. Petit fours toppled from a tiered plate.

Brinks staggered, balled his fist, and drew back his arm.

Sven stepped up, grabbed Brinks' arm with both hands, and bent it behind his back.

Papa, Toby, George Harris, Joseph Marew, Henry Pinchin, and Big Toby joined Sven and forcefully removed Brinks from the hall.

Flora rushed to Charles. "I'm so sorry! Are you all right?"

Still bent over, he began to straighten, taking a deep breath. "He knocked the wind out of me is all . . . *and* my pride." He glanced about the floor. "You haven't seen it anywhere, have you?"

Flora chuckled. "I'm sure it will show up soon."

Charles reached for her, his gentle gaze meeting hers. "Are *you* all right?"

She was about to place her hand in his and offer a reassuring squeeze when Lillian pressed between them. "Charles, did that horrible man harm you? If he did, I'm going to—"

"No harm done, Lillian."

She smoothed her hand over his topcoat, inspecting the backside. "Your coat—it's all stained with punch and petit fours!" She dabbed at it with her handkerchief.

Leaving Charles to Lillian, Flora turned to the damaged refreshment table. Where should she begin to set things aright?

Mrs. J.B. Kitchen and the elder Mrs. Harris came up on either side of her, each in turn expressing their concern.

"That Brinks fellow had his nerve, coming in here and treating you like he did. Are you all right, dear?" Mrs. Kitchen regarded her with careful scrutiny.

"Dr. Bellows is right over there." Mrs. Harris pointed across the room. "I'll get him if you like."

"No need. I'm fine." Flora offered a reassuring smile.

Shoving broken cups beneath the table with her foot, Mrs. Harris continued. "I just knew from the moment that saloon opened, it would mean nothing but trouble for us all." She gave one more shove with her foot. "I'm going to get a broom and dust pan."

Flora had begun helping Mrs. Kitchen to right the tipped-over punch cups when Lavinia, Mama, and Elin surrounded her, fussing over her and lending hands to the clean-up effort. Within moments Mrs. Harris and Marian Phillips appeared with a broom and dustpan to sweep up the broken crystal. Then Maggie Coughlin, the seamstress, approached Flora.

"I heard a ripping sound when Mr. Brinks stepped on your train." She lifted Flora's train to inspect the tear caused by Brinks' boot. "I have a needle and thread in the cloakroom. Let's go and repair it right now, while the others are cleaning up here."

Maggie made quick work of the mending job and they emerged from the cloakroom just as those who had ousted Brinks from the hall came inside. Sven took a path directly to Flora, his brows narrowed, his words clipped.

"Are you all right?"

Flora nodded. "No need to worry about me. I'm fine." She darted a glance in the direction of the refreshment table. "And it looks like everything is back to apple-pie order over there, too." No sooner had she said the words than the orchestra began to play. "I believe this is the dance that you and I promised to Lillian and Charles."

Spotting the other couple near the end of the hall, Sven escorted Flora there. With longing, she watched him pair off with Lillian. Then she faced Charles once again for the opening curtsey and bow.

Much to Flora's delight, Charles proved to be the perfect partner for the rapid step-slide action of the gallop. With confidence and grace, he held her firmly enough to give adequate support, and moved across the floor in perfect synchronization with the beat of the music. In no time at all, it seemed, they were offering each other the closing curtsey and bow.

"Thank you, Miss McAdams. After that dance with you, I'm beginning to think that this evening will turn out all right, after all." Charles smiled broadly.

"I believe it will, Mr. Mason. I believe it will." With a smile, she turned to find Joseph Marew ready to serve as her partner for the polka, just as he had promised.

Dance followed dance, partner followed partner in smooth transition. But no matter who was leading Flora around the dance floor, she made a point to find Sven in the crowd. And when she did, her heart yearned to be the one held in his arms.

As the time for the final waltz with Sven drew near, Flora silently thanked God for this special evening. It had offered a side to life and insight to those with whom she danced that she had never before experienced. The people she knew best—her brother, father, brother-in-law, and Dr. Bellows— regarded her with a courtesy she had not known until tonight. And the fellows who had been mere acquaintances or casual friends now viewed her with new interest. When couples had gathered around the refreshment table to sample the dainty pastries and sip the fruity punch, manners and conversation had reached a higher level of civility than Flora had ever witnessed in this rough and dirty pig iron town.

Such thoughts vanished when the music stopped and Mr. Powell announced that the time for raffling off the stove had arrived. Henry Pinchin carried a firkin containing the tickets to the center of the dance floor. The elder Mrs. Harris was invited to draw out a ticket, which she handed to Mr. Powell. A violinist drew his bow across the strings with a flourish, and Mr. Powell announced that William Pinchin, Henry's father, was the winner. Polite applause rippled across the room, and Flora again thought how much more exciting would be her drawing for the sleigh, held at the school after the Christmas program with the whole town in attendance. Those thoughts took flight at the opening strain to the final waltz.

Flora curtsied to Sven's bow and he took her into his arms. The strength of his embrace, the warmth of his hand enclosing hers, and the gentle essence of bay rum in his hair so distracted her that she almost forgot the steps of the dance. But before her feet tangled with his, she remembered the left foot front—right foot pivot—left foot front pattern. Almost as one, they stepped and turned to the rhythm and flow of Strauss's *Blue Danube*, and Flora's heart soared to new heights on winged notes of the violins.

Too soon, the melodic strains died away. Retrieving her cloak, she placed her arm in Sven's for the walk home, stung by the brisk wind and beleaguered by the reality that the gorgeous event was now over, reduced to nothing more than a mere memory. At the door, Sven kissed her hand and bid her good night, disappearing into the darkness like a phantom. For a moment, she stood on the doorstep wondering if her fairytale had even been real. Then she remembered the start of the evening when Sven was standing in the exact same spot, looking at her as if he'd never seen her before.

With a laugh, she opened the door and went inside to recount her experiences to Grandma, who despite the lateness of the hour, insisted on learning every detail of the evening.

CHAPTER 23

Flora arose later than usual the next morning, thoughts of Sven swimming in her head.

The voices of Violet, Dan, and Rose, and the patter of their feet scampering about the first floor played the overture to a new day. The zinnias that Sven had brought her added a splash of color to her dresser top where Grandma had thoughtfully placed them, assuring a bright and beautiful start to her morning.

Flora lifted the lid of her trunk, pulled out the troll Sven had given her a couple of days ago, and studied him.

"How I wish you could talk, and tell me of the man, the family, and the place where you came from." With a dreamy sigh, she carefully hid him away again.

At her wash stand, she splashed her face with water and toweled dry, certain that by the time she had gotten dressed, she would be too late for breakfast. But when she walked into the dining room, Grandma, Mama, Lavinia, and Huck were still lingering over cups of coffee. Grandma quickly fried eggs and bacon for Flora.

While she ate, Huck spoke of the previous night's events.

"Mark my words. That ball will go down in the history of Fayette as the encounter between the beauty and the Brinks—I mean the beast!" He chuckled, a lock of wavy red hair falling over his forehead.

Flora sighed. "I hope you're wrong. That's the only part of the evening I'm eager to forget. Certainly there must be a more pleasant topic we can discuss."

"I can think of one." Mama grinned. "I've been trying to persuade your sister and brother-in-law to stay another night so they can attend Mr. Powell's auction at the Company Store this afternoon. Papa's going to meet me there when he gets off work. I hope there will still be some good bargains left."

"Mr. Powell picked a right smart time to start his auction," said Grandma. "At four o'clock he'll get the night shift before they go to work and the day shift when they get out at five."

"I didn't know about the auction," said Flora, "not that I have any money to spend."

"Neither do we," said Lavinia. "Thank you for your invitation, Mother, but our brood is heading home right after lunch. Goodness knows there's plenty of work waiting for me there." She rose and carried her dirty dishes to the kitchen.

When Flora finished eating, the children were more than willing to help her feed and water Pet and Big Boy and take them for a walk. Down Stewart Avenue they went, the trio of redheaded youngsters leading the way.

Flora relished the warm sunshine on her face, the mild temperature, and the soft breeze that had replaced the threatening skies, chilling winds, and stormy waters of the previous day. As they circled the hotel and turned up Sheldon Avenue, Big Toby came out the back door to greet them, shaking hands with each of the children, offering affection to the dogs, and reminiscing enthusiastically about the ball. He had headed back to the hotel when he suddenly turned and called out.

"Miss Flora, you're going to the auction, aren't ya? Everybody's gonna be there."

"I guess so." If Big Toby were right, she wouldn't mind running into Sven.

Children and dogs in tow, Flora headed up Sheldon, and around Cedar Lane. They were almost home when Pet grew unusually agitated over a small, terrier-like stray he had spotted several feet away in a stand of cedars. The dog was a female, and Pet's behavior reminded Flora that she must enlist Dr. Bellows' aid as soon as possible to perform the surgery on Pet that would prevent him from fathering pups.

At home, Flora held a morning tea party with Violet and Rose. A while later, the entire family squeezed around the table for a pleasant midday dinner.

When Flora had bid good-bye to her sister's family, she headed upstairs for an afternoon nap. As much as she hated to admit it, her recovery from the flu followed so closely by the excitement of the ball and the late evening out had made her more tired than usual. A couple of hours in bed restored her energy, and she awoke eager to assist Mama and Grandma with the remaining Saturday chores and accompany them to the auction.

They arrived half an hour before the bidding was to start. Wagons and buggies lined the streets, and a large throng had gathered in front of the Company Store where men's work apparel, boots, and tools covered tables that had been carried outside. Charles Mason was looking over the merchandise, and so was Lillian Ruggles, along with Papa. Not far from them stood Dr. Bellows. Flora headed straight for him.

"Dr. Bellows, I need your help. Pet is getting far too interested in becoming a father."

The good doctor smiled. "We were going to cure him of that notion just about the time you took sick, weren't we?"

Flora nodded.

Stroking his beard, the doctor grew thoughtful. "What are you doing after supper tonight?"

"Curing Pet of the fathering notion, I hope."

"Bring him to me at seven o'clock. It won't take more than half an hour."

"See you then. Thanks, Dr. Bellows." She turned to go, nearly bumping into Charles Mason.

"Hello, Miss McAdams." He smiled broadly beneath his dark, neatly trimmed mustache.

"Good afternoon, Mr. Mason." Flora looked around for Lillian and caught sight of her on her father's arm heading for their buggy.

"It's good we crossed paths, Miss McAdams. I want to tell you once again how much I enjoyed our dance together last night."

"I'm glad to hear it. I enjoyed it, too." Flora looked for Mama and Grandma, spotting them at the next table. "If you'll excuse me, Mama and Grandma are probably wondering where I've run off to."

"Are they here, too? I must say hello." He went with her, his congenial manner putting everyone at ease and causing minutes to pass more quickly than Flora realized. In no time, the bidding had begun and the first half of the auction had come to a conclusion, marked by the whistle that released the day shift from their duties and called the night shift to work.

Papa and Toby joined them. Charles got along with them just as easily as he had with Mama and Grandma. But his gaze and his conversation never strayed from Flora for long. Though she enjoyed his attention, she kept rising up on tiptoe, looking in the direction of the Machine Shop to see if Sven might emerge.

Suddenly, he was right beside her, stepping between her and Charles as he turned toward Mama and Papa.

"Mr. McAdams, Mrs. McAdams, I ask permission. May I call on your daughter this evening?"

CHAPTER 24

Flora held her breath as Papa considered Sven's request to call on her.

Charles Mason remained nearby, obviously interested in the response.

Papa's gaze met Mama's.

She nodded.

Papa turned to Sven. "You have *our* permission to call on Flora. The question is do you have *hers?*"

Sven's gaze met Flora's, his brow cocked.

She offered a smile so wide it nearly made her lips crack. "I look forward to seeing you. Is half-past seven all right? I have a small matter to attend to at Dr. Bellows' at seven, but I should be home by half-past."

Sven nodded. And when he showed no indication that he was about to leave, Charles Mason disappeared in the crowd.

~~~

As planned, at half-past seven, Flora emerged from Dr. Bellows' carrying the blanket-wrapped Pet still under the influence of Powers and Weightman Sulphate of Morphine. No sooner had the door closed behind her than a hatted figure emerged from the dusky shadows.

Hair stood up on the back of her neck. And then she recognized Sven.

"I walk you home." Carefully, he took Pet from her arms, his expression solemn. "Will he live?"

"He'll be a little sore, is all. But in the future, he won't be contributing to the problem of too many dogs in this town."

Sven nodded.

Nothing more was said until they entered the back door and stepped into Grandma's room.

Grandma was sitting in her rocker tatting. A smile lit her face as she gazed up at Flora and Sven. "Mr. Jorgenson, nice to see you."

He nodded. "Good evening."

Grandma's smile disappeared. "I see you've brought Pet inside."

Flora moved closer. "I'm hoping you'll let us lay him on the floor here in your room and keep watch over him until he recovers from the morphine Dr. Bellows gave him in order to do the surgery. The warmth of your stove would be so much better for his recovery than the cold night air."

A silent moment lapsed, and then she drew a deep breath. "All right. Just this once. Now, can I get you some tea and cookies?"

"That would be wonderful. I'll help." Flora started to follow her out of the room.

Grandma put up her hand. "You stay right here. Why don't you add a stick of wood to the stove, and leave the rest to me?"

"Yes, Grandma, and thank you." She offered a quick hug.

Within minutes Grandma returned with tea and sugar cookies and sat with them making quiet conversation. For over an hour, chatter ranged from the Lindbergs' kin who had finally arrived from Sweden, to the fascination amongst fellows in the area with the pool tables at Harris's where Toby was spending his evening, to the new cases of flu she had heard about in the village.

At half-past nine Pet stirred, then lay his head down and slept again until ten. Rising on shaky legs, he gazed about as if uncertain as to his location. Flora quickly ushered him out the back door followed by Sven, who carried a lantern.

The sound of the back door closing woke Big Boy, who issued loud warning barks until calmed by Flora's reassurances. Pet relieved himself, lapped up a few swallows of water from his bowl, and settled in his kennel, ready to sleep some more.

Sven turned down the lantern and set it aside. Taking each of Flora's hands in his, he gazed at her, a semi-smile curving the corners of his mouth.

Flora studied the look in Sven's eyes and tried to plumb its depths. Unable to fathom the emotions hidden there, she cherished the more apparent signs of his feelings—the warmth and strength of his hands enfolding hers, his concern for the animals that she loved, and his desire to spend the evening with her doing nothing more than watching a sleeping dog.

Sven released Flora and picked up the lantern. "I must thank your grandmother, then go. Morning comes early." He walked her to the back door and stepped inside long enough to return the lantern and express his gratitude for tea, cookies, and conversation. Then he disappeared into the night leaving Flora sorry that their time together had come to an end.

Grandma rose from her rocking chair and reached for the tray of dirty cups, saucers, and plates. "Your folks have already turned in. I'd better do the same. But I'm going to wash up these dishes and set the breakfast table first."

"Let me help, Grandma." Flora took the tray from her and carried it to the kitchen. She had set the dirty dishes in a basin and was filling it with warm, soapy water when Toby returned from his evening at Harris's pool hall.

Blue tweed cap still covering his thick hair, he headed straight for the cookie jar, his words casual "I met Sven going down toward town. Did he just leave here?"

Flora nodded. "He left a couple of minutes ago. The way he spoke, I thought he was going back to Lindbergs' to turn in. 'Morning comes early,' he said. Why would he tell me that if he was going to town?"

"I'm sure he had his reason," said Grandma. "Maybe he thought of something he needed to check on at the Machine Shop."

Toby cocked his brow. "Or maybe he went to check on something in another location. Something with pretty curves."

"Good glory!" Flora exclaimed. "Who could that be?"

Toby only smiled, shrugged his broad shoulders, and took another bite of cookie.

Grandma shook her finger at Toby. "Stop teasing your sister. And for goodness sake, take off that cap. It's not polite to wear a hat indoors." To Flora, she said, "I think the right question is *what* could have pretty curves. And the only reasonable answer is—"

"The sleigh!" Flora concluded. "Mr. Jorgensen went to check on the sleigh, didn't he Toby?"

A gleam in his eyes, he shoved the last of the cookie into his mouth, brushed the crumbs off his hands, pulled off his cap, and headed for the hall tree in the front entryway.

Flora turned to Grandma. "That brother of mine can be such a tease. And as for the sleigh, my curiosity is killing me. I'm dying to know where it is and see what it looks like."

Grandma offered a warning look. "If you know what's good for you, you'll put that sleigh from your mind. It would break Mr. Jorgensen's heart if you spoiled his surprise by getting a look at it before it's finished. Now get busy with those dishes. It's growing later by the minute."

~~~

Morning dawned, bringing an end to a curious night of dreams about Sven, the sleigh, and Pet. Flora fed and watered her dogs and let them out of their kennels for a few minutes. Pet had perked up considerably, and appeared to be recovering on schedule. She silently thanked God for watching over the beloved creature as she walked with Mama and Grandma to the church service held at the school. As usual, mostly women and children filled the seats, since Sundays were a day of work just like the other six for the employees of the Jackson Iron Company. Only when the furnace shut down for repairs and maintenance were some of the day shift men free to attend services.

Flora had missed church services during her bout with the flu, and she was thankful to hear the Word of God preached again. But throughout the minister's message, and even while she was singing hymns, Sven was ever on her mind. She found herself wondering what church had been like for him in Norway and in Canada where he had lived before moving to Fayette. And she wondered many other things about him, too—his hopes, his fears, his plans, his dreams. Only time and a deepening friendship would reveal the answers.

By the time the service ended, the sun had cast tourmalines across the ripples on the harbor and a gentle breeze had chased away fall clouds to usher in blue skies and reminiscences of late summer temperatures. How Flora wished she could spend a day as glorious as this with Sven, but his work demanded otherwise. And so with thankfulness for the beauty of the day and thoughts of Sven her constant companions, she helped Mama and

Grandma prepare and serve the midday meal. A stroll with Big Boy followed by Bible reading and a nap consumed the remainder of the afternoon.

When the five o'clock whistle blew, she envisioned Sven heading for Lindbergs' to take supper and longed with all her heart to spend the evening with him, but no such plan was in the offing. With vain attempts to put her mind elsewhere, she helped Mama and Grandma with supper dishes, then donned her straw hat and headed out the door to leash Big Boy for an evening stroll. She was halfway to his kennel when she saw Sven's tall, sturdy form coming her way.

CHAPTER 25

Flora greeted Sven with a smile. "Mr. Jorgensen, what brings you here on this fine summer-like eve?"

"Before I answer, I must ask. Please. Call me Sven. It is the way of my friends. Are we not friends?"

Flora wanted to say he was far more than a friend to her but such an admission must wait. "Yes, Sven, we are friends. So you will call me Flora."

He nodded and then glanced at the leash in her hand. "Now I tell you what brings me here, Flora. On this fine evening I come to ask, may I take you for a walk—you and your dog?"

"Please do."

Big Boy bounded out of his kennel and tugged hard at the end of his leash until reminded to heel. When he had calmed down enough to stay at Flora's side, they took a route down Stewart Avenue, across town, and up the bluff trail. Soon, they came to the ruts where the sleigh had stood. Sven passed them by with neither a glance nor a word, but Flora had to call upon all the restraint she could muster to keep a torrent of questions from spilling forth.

Farther along, they arrived at the old tree stump in the opening where the bay was visible. Sven paused to gaze out across Snail-Shell Harbor to the setting sun beyond. He seemed deep in thought.

"Are you thinking about your family in Norway and the Atlantic coast near the farm where you grew up?"

He offered an enigmatic smile. "That and other things." He reached for her hand. "I take you home now."

He held her hand firmly in his. While Flora's feet traversed grassy trail and gravel streets, her heart hovered somewhere in the heavens above and plans for an evening in the parlor with Sven took shape in her mind. She would serve tea and cookies and challenge him to a game of Botticelli. But when she invited him to come inside, he shook his head.

"I must go. More work waits for me. Good night." As quickly as he had appeared, he disappeared down Stewart Avenue.

Flora's heart sank like a deflated balloon. She unleashed and kenneled Big Boy while Pet whined for attention. She let him out of his kennel and lavished affection on him, then checked the site of his surgery. It was healing well without any sign of infection. She breathed a prayer of thanks, returned him to his kennel, and brought both dogs fresh water and their last meal of the day.

Images of Sven and their walk on the bluff were still fresh in her mind when she went inside for the last time, finding Grandma in her room, shoulders stooped over her sewing. Without looking up, she said, "I'm glad you're back. This house is too quiet when I'm here alone."

"Where is everyone?"

"Angus said it was too fine an evening to sit inside, so he took your mother for a walk."

"Is Toby with Elin?"

Grandma shook her head. "He tried to see her, but she's busy with her kin from Sweden. He ate a sugar cookie, then he left, mumbling something about work to be done."

"On the sleigh?"

Grandma shrugged and put down her sewing. "Tell me about your walk with Mr. Jorgensen. Why didn't you invite him in?"

"Our walk was *wonderful!* And I *did* invite him in. He said, 'More work waits for me,' then he headed toward town. Do you suppose he's working on the sleigh, he and Toby?"

"I couldn't say. Where did you go on your walk?" She picked up her sewing again.

"The bluff. The view was beautiful, as usual. The lake seems to go on forever there, you know. You can see the harbor and the furnace and the Superintendent's house very clearly, and Sand Bay and Burnt Bluff in the distance. Then, the water just stretches out to the horizon." She closed her eyes and recalled the enchantment of the view, and Sven beside her.

After a few dreamy moments, her eyes opened again and for the first time, she took notice of the garment

Grandma was sewing. "What is it that you're making, Grandma?"

"A work shirt for your father. You can help. I have a sleeve in need of a cuff, and a needle all threaded." She pulled the items out of the sewing basket beside her chair and handed them to Flora.

Her first instinct was to hand them back, but it had always bothered her that she had failed in her attempt to mend Sven's shirt. With the somewhat disheartening thought that her stitches could always be removed and done over if she failed again, she took needle in hand and began to sew.

~~~

Oil can in one hand and rag in the other, Sven methodically filled the oiling cups of the steam engine, thinking about Flora as he worked. The view from the bluff and her question as to whether it reminded him of Norway had made him realize anew how much he missed the fiord and the mountains, and how powerfully they pulled at his heart. He had left his beloved country with a plan to make his fortune and return home, there to improve his standing both as a farmer and in the social ranks of the area where he would seek a bride.

But life on this side of the ocean had gone far differently from what he had imagined. He had earned a nice wage in Canada and was earning a better wage here at Fayette. Nevertheless, he had not become wealthy. He would not be returning to Norway for many more years, if ever. That fact pained him deeply. But he must accept it and move on.

As he wiped oil from the flywheel, he was determined to wipe unhappy reflections from his mind and return to thoughts of Flora. A fly buzzed about his head, distracting him and threatening to land and bite. Setting down the oil can, he snapped at the pest with his oily rag, knocked it to the floor and crushed it with his foot.

Then he tossed the rag aside with a laugh, reminded of his very first encounter with the tenacious Miss McAdams, when he had snapped a rag at her dog. Sitting on his stool, chin in hand, he looked back on the past few days. Though the brisk, cold winds of fall sometimes rattled the shutters and nipped at the remaining zinnias, his friendship with Flora mimicked the warmth of this unseasonably fine day, budding as if the May sun were upon them. And if he were to be completely honest with himself, he must admit that only when he was with her, or in the shed working on the sleigh that she planned to raffle off, was he able to put dreams of the Old Country to rest.

But a future on this side of the ocean would take planning. And before his friendship with Flora came into full blossom, there were things he must know. He offered a prayer of gratitude and supplication to the Almighty. Then, bolting the Machine Shop door behind him, he headed for the shed and the sleigh.

Flora's brother was already at work sanding the new wood on the body. Sven joined in the labor without comment until Toby spoke.

"Sven, I know you're not from Sweden, but . . . I'm thinking that maybe the Norwegian girls aren't too much different from the Swedish ones, and I sure could use some advice."

Sven offered a nod of encouragement, certain that by this night's end, his own questions about Flora and her family would receive the very best of answers.

CHAPTER 26

Saturday Morning
October 25

The crisp breeze chased crunchy leaves across the ground and the sun struggled to find its way past clouds of gray as Flora stepped out onto Stewart Avenue to walk Pet and Big Boy. She hadn't gone far when Dr. Bellows and Superintendent J.B. Kitchen came toward her leading an uncooperative sheep by the halter. Her dogs barked and she pulled them off to the side of the road to let the others pass.

When both gentlemen had greeted her, Dr. Bellows said, "If you can spare a few minutes when you're done walking, please stop by my place. I could sure use your assistance with this pitiful creature."

"I'll be there in twenty minutes." Flora continued on her way, wondering why that sheep was so unwilling to follow, and what Dr. Bellows had in mind for the animal.

~~~

Saturday Morning
November 1

Flora released Superintendent Kitchen's sheep into the pen with the rest of the flock, pleased at how well it had healed from the surgery she and Dr. Bellows had performed on its head last week for parasites. The two small incisions near the ears had drained and healed without infection and it appeared that, after a week of recovery in her back yard, it was ready to resume a normal healthy life, none the worse for the procedure.

She watched it for a few minutes as it began to graze, and seeing nothing amiss in its behavior, thanked the Almighty for the successful outcome, and headed down Furnace Hill toward home, looking forward to the visit from her sister's family later in the day. It would be good to see Lavinia, Huck and the children again. She hadn't seen them since they had come for the ball a month ago. Her pace quickened as she remembered her conversation with Mama at breakfast, and the chores to be completed before the arrival of Lavinia's family.

By the time supper was ready to go on the table, the chores had been completed, the aroma of baked ham wafted from the kitchen, and the house was a-buzz with the happy voices and scampering feet of Violet, Dan, and Rose. When everyone had gathered at the table, the blessing had been asked, and plates had been filled with ham, potatoes, peas, and cornbread, Mama inquired of the children's progress with their education. Violet reported perfect grades in reading and writing. Dan told proudly of his achievements in ciphering, and Rose, who was still too young to attend school with her older siblings, recited the entire alphabet without error or hesitation.

Mama smiled broadly, complimenting and encouraging each child. Then Papa directed the conversation to more adult topics of local interest.

"There's been a thief afoot in the village this week. First, he took John Chaulklin's overcoat, then Joe Harris came up missing a pair of new trousers."

Huck laughed, his blue eyes twinkling. "I don't know a living soul who is man enough to wear Joe Harris's pants. Any idea who the culprit is?"

Papa shook his balding head.

"He was smart enough to steal without getting caught, but," Toby paused, and with a shrug of his broad shoulders, continued, "if he's from around here, I don't see how he's going to make use of stolen clothing without it being recognized."

"Maybe he's got some kind of operation going where he sells it to out-of-towners," Huck said.

Mama set down her tea cup. "I don't know about operations of such a scurrilous nature, but Flora has been busy with operations of a beneficial sort since you saw her last."

Grandma frowned. "Goodness sakes, Mary. Discussion of those animals is hardly fit for dinner table conversation."

Lavinia laughed, her brown eyes merry. "Grandma, by now, we're all quite accustomed to talk of Flora's work with the creatures hereabouts." To Flora, she said,

"Tell me what you've been up to since we were here for the ball."

"This week I've been caring for one of Superintendent Kitchen's sheep that Dr. Bellows and I operated on last Saturday for parasites. He made a full recovery and returned to his flock this morning. Then, two weeks ago I had Mr. Ferris's dog, Max, here for surgery. Earlier this week, Mr. Ferris told me that Max is doing better than ever."

Huck's gaze met Flora's. "What was wrong with the animal?"

Flora cleared her throat, glanced at the children who seemed to be too busy chasing peas around their plates to be listening, and replied discreetly, "He had a habit of running after the girl dogs."

"Flora wants to cure all the boy dogs in the village of that habit," said Toby. "She wants to make them all like Pet and Big Boy, but Mr. Ferris is the only one who actually let her do it."

Grandma sighed. "Can't we speak of something more pleasant?"

Huck smiled. "Grandma, this is a mighty delicious dinner your hands have prepared. The ham is tender and tasty, the mashed potatoes are smooth and creamy, and the cornbread is . . . deliciously corny."

The adults laughed, especially Grandma, who set her gaze on Huck. "You always did have the gift of blarney and I see you haven't lost it."

Dan offered his father a puzzled look. "Papa, what's blarney?"

Huck smiled. "Talk, son. Grandma means I'm good at talking."

The little boy nodded and went back to work on his mashed potatoes.

Mama focused on Huck. "Your compliment on the ham makes me wonder. Shall we serve that again for Thanksgiving, or shall we roast a nice, fat turkey?"

A unanimous vote for turkey quickly settled the issue.

Papa stroked his clean-shaven chin. "On the subject of turkey, I understand quite a number of local fellows are planning to participate in the turkey shoot on Thanksgiving Day."

Flora's heart sank. "Good glory, what is the point? How much sport is there in tying a turkey to a target and taking aim at it from a few feet with a shotgun? Better to chop off its head and end its life quickly than to terrorize it by tying it down and blasting away at it. I ought to have a talk with each of those Gun Club fellows and deliver a piece of my mind on the topic."

Toby shook his head. "I wouldn't do that if I were you, Flora. Those Gun Club fellows are the ones who work the hardest on your sleigh."

She drew a breath to protest further but Papa's words stopped her.

"Toby is right, Flora. If you know what's good for you—and your friendship with Mr. Jorgensen—you'll say nothing."

"Yes, Papa." Despite her agreement, her heart ached for the birds that would become targets.

Lavinia's gaze met Flora's. "By the way, how *is* that friendship with Mr. Jorgensen getting on? He certainly seemed taken with you on the night of the ball."

Grandma smiled. "From all appearances, it's getting on famously. He helps her walk the dogs several times a week."

Huck's brow rose. "You must be learning a lot about the Norwegians after spending so much time together."

Flora chuckled. "Your knowledge of the Norwegians is sadly lacking, my dear brother-in-law, but I'll enlighten you. Unlike the Irish, they do not possess the gift of blarney. In fact, I've failed miserably in getting Sven to speak of his family or his home in Norway."

"It must be the difference in weather," Huck conjectured. "Norway is probably so cold most of the time that the citizens are reluctant to waste warm breath on conversation."

"It isn't that cold *here,*" Flora wryly observed.

"I've spent many an evening with Sven working on the sleigh," said Toby, "and he's said barely a word about himself, let alone his family or home back in the Old Country. It's just his way."

"He probably misses his kin and his old home," said Grandma, "and talking about them just makes him miss them more, so he says nothing."

"Maybe so," said Papa, "but I believe it's a case of Sven being a lot more work than he is talk. And that's not a bad thing in this town."

"I'm sure Mr. Jorgensen will speak of his family and his homeland when he's ready," said Lavinia. "Just be patient, Flora. Now, going back to Huck's mention of the cold, I noticed that Pet and Big Boy are allowed in Grandma's room now. Is that because of the cold weather coming on?"

Mama nodded. "Flora's been training very hard with those two dogs, teaching them proper indoor behavior. She's taught them to stay in her room at night and to lie quietly in Mother's room during mealtime."

"What happens during the rest of the day?" Huck asked.

Grandma frowned. "They follow me from room to room, begging for attention."

Lavinia laughed. "Kind of like children."

At her mention of children, Violet, Dan, and Rose spoke in turn.

"Mama, I'm full. May I be excused, please?"

"Me, too, Mama?"

"Me, too?"

"You may all be excused as soon as you have finished what's on your plates."

They stabbed their forks at the remaining morsels on their plates, making claims over who would finish first.

While conversation turned to Sac Bay news, Flora's mind drifted back to Lavinia's comment that Sven would speak of his family and homeland when he was ready, and that she simply must be patient. Silently, she petitioned the Almighty for the grace to do her part.

Late that night, when she was ready to go to bed, she paused to take the troll from her trunk. Gazing into its ugly but endearing face, she wondered again what it would tell her if it could speak. Then she knelt beside her bed and thanked God for the blessings of the day, adding, "I sure would be grateful if you could see fit to get Sven to talk more. Amen."

~~~

The following evening
Sunday, November 2

With daylight fading fast, Flora pulled on her cloak, leashed the dogs and headed out the door for her evening walk. As often happened, Sven, clad in his brown hat and jacket, emerged from the boarding house to join her, taking Big Boy's leash in hand while she walked Pet. And as usual, with Sven's one- or two-word answers to her questions about his day, the burden of conversation fell to Flora.

"Mild weather we've had today. Sunshine, barely a breeze, and not especially cold. I can't help wondering if it was like this in Norway in early November?" She bit her lip. She had promised herself not to bring up Norway or Sven's family, but to follow Lavinia's advice and wait until Sven was ready. Yet the question had slipped off her tongue.

"It is colder there by now, with snow, and the days are shorter."

There it was again. Sven slipping back into silence. But Flora could tell by his pensive look and the slight flexing of his jaw that he was pondering something far more serious than the difference in weather between Fayette and his home across the ocean. She pressed her lips together, determined to ask nothing further though she yearned desperately to know more.

Conversation stalled though the walk progressed all the way down Stewart Avenue, around the village and back along Sheldon Avenue and around Cedar Lane.

When they arrived at Flora's front step, she reached for Big Boy's leash.

Sven refused to release it. "Don't go in. Not yet."

His clipped words put her on edge. And though darkness had fallen, enough light spilled from the front parlor window for her to read the anxious look on his face. Before she could ask what was troubling him, he spoke again.

"Many times you ask about my family. The truth is hard. My family is poor. My father worked day and night. Still, he could not get ahead. I pestered him to take a loan. A neighbor backed it. But he could not write his name. My father signed for him. Then the neighbor changed his mind. My father was found guilty of forgery. But when the sheriff came to take him to prison, he found my father hanging dead in the barn. All because of me. That is when I decided it is far better to be free in a strange land than a slave at home. Now you know the truth. Maybe you don't want to be my friend." He shoved the leash at her and turned to go.

Flora caught him by the sleeve. "Wait! I *do* want to be your friend!"

He turned back, his expression just short of a smile.

Flora rushed on. "I'm so sorry about your father. I can see that his loss was a terrible blow to you—still is. But I want you to know that it doesn't make any difference to me how poor you were, or how your father died. We're friends now, and . . . good glory, that means much more to me than all your troubles of the past."

He took her firmly by the hand and looked straight into her eyes. "I am glad. Very glad." With a little squeeze and a promise to see her again very soon, he released her and disappeared into the darkness.

A few minutes later, in her room, she took the troll out of the trunk, sat on her bed, and stared into its odd face. "Sven's secret is out. And from now on, so are you. Whenever I look at you, I will remember to say a little prayer that God will heal his heart from the hurts of the past." She propped the troll against her pillow and knelt by her bed to pray.

CHAPTER 27

Monday Evening
November 3

Her heart pounding, Flora stood at Superintendent
J.B. Kitchen's front door while Dr. Bellows knocked.
Inside, his King Charles spaniel barked. His dog, and
dozens of others like him in the village, were contributing to the excess number of dogs. After a month of
trying, Flora had managed to convince only Mr. Ferris,
the barn boss, to allow her to perform the surgery that
would prevent his dog from fathering puppies. At Dr.
Bellows' suggestion and arrangement, she had come to
Superintendent Kitchen's home to discuss the matter
with him. If she could convince him to agree to the surgery on his spaniel, others in the town would be more
likely to view the operation favorably. Silently, she
thanked God for helping her to save the Kitchens' sheep
that had suffered from hydatid, then she asked Him for
the right words to successfully make her point about
their dog.

The door opened, and the matronly housekeeper welcomed them with a smile. "Dr. Bellows, Miss McAdams, do come in. Mr. Kitchen is expecting you." She led them to the parlor on the left where pale blue plaster walls, panel curtains of white sheer and lace, and an oriental carpet coordinated nicely with the burgundy velvet love seat and three matching chairs positioned against the walls of the modestly sized room.

J.B. Kitchen, his dark hair and beard meticulously groomed, stood when they entered, offering handshakes and pleasantries while his dog ran circles around their feet, yapping. When they had been seated and the chestnut and white spaniel had taken a place on his master's lap, the superintendent focused on Flora.

"I understand you have a matter of importance you wish to discuss with me."

"Yes, sir. It's about the dogs in this village. There are way too many of them. And more unwanted puppies are being born all the time. Dr. Bellows has offered a suggestion for reducing the number of unwanted dogs, and I'm more than willing to act on it, if only I could convince people to go along with it." She paused. How could she delicately explain her plan?

"Speak on, Miss McAdams."

"Sir, you are undoubtedly familiar with the method used by farmers to turn a stallion into a gelding or a bull into an ox. I believe if I were to apply this same procedure to dogs of the heartier gender in this town, we would have far fewer strays and unwanted puppies. With the good doctor's help, I have already rendered my own two dogs incapable of fathering puppies. I performed the

surgery on Mr. Ferris's dog as well, and there has been
no ill effect on any of the three dogs. They are just as
happy and healthy as if they had never had the surgery.
In fact, Mr. Ferris thinks his dog is a much nicer pet
now, more content and less given to roaming."

Superintendent Kitchen, brow raised, turned to Dr.
Bellows with a smile. "I didn't know you'd been apply-
ing your surgical skills to dogs, C. J."

Dr. Bellows nodded. "As Miss McAdams has said,
they're none the worse off for it. But there is one problem." He turned to Flora. "Tell J.B. about it."

She continued. "Even though Dr. Bellows and I have
had excellent results with the surgeries, I have not been
able to win my point with the vast majority of dog owners. Dr. Bellows suggested that if I could get the most
respected citizen of the town to set the example, others
would be more open to my suggestion. That's why I'm
hoping you will let me operate on your spaniel to prevent
him from fathering puppies and adding to the excess
number of dogs that already make Fayette their home."

The superintendent cast a protective look at the dog
snuggled in his lap. Then his gaze met Flora's. "Your
idea may be a good one, and it may work as you say, but
it sounds a good deal too bothersome to me. What's
wrong with the old ways? If you want to get rid of a
stray, shoot it. If you want to get rid of a litter of puppies, drown them."

Flora cringed. "With all due respect, sir, those methods treat only the results of the problem, not the cause. If
I operate on your dog, a good number of the other dog
owners in this village will go along with my plan.

Fayette will be a much pleasanter place in which to live. And one thing more. I *did* see your spaniel dancing with a stray lady mongrel down on Harbor Street just last week. There's no doubt he's done his part in contributing to the town's overabundance of dogs."

"Zippy? You don't say?" J.B. regarded his dog with a look that combined disapproval with respect.

Flora prayed as the superintendent cradled the spaniel in his arms and wandered to the window. A glance at Dr. Bellows garnered her a look of encouragement. A moment later, the superintendent faced them again, his gaze on Flora.

"Miss McAdams, I like your pluck. I certainly approve of the work you've been doing with the animals in this town, and I'm very appreciative that you were able to save my sheep, but . . ." He paused to gaze affectionately at Zippy.

Flora wanted to tell him that much of the work she'd done with the dogs in the village had been necessitated by the fact that there were too many of them running loose. She drew a breath to say so, but he continued.

"What I'm trying to say is that it just isn't easy for me to think of you operating on Zippy. But it's the right thing to do." He came to her and placed the spaniel in her arms. "I'll do my part, and I hope from now on, many others will do their part, too."

"Thank you, Mr. Kitchen, thank you! I'll return Zippy to you in a couple of days, none the worse for his surgery, I promise." She shifted the dog to her left arm in order to offer her hand, and with a hearty shake, she and Dr. Bellows took their leave.

~~~

Two weeks later
Thanksgiving Day Evening

"Mama, may we decorate the gingerbread house now?" Violet wanted to know.

"Please, Mama?" Dan asked.

"Please, Mama?" Rose echoed.

Lavinia smiled down at her children. "Yes, you may, but first, go out to the well and wash your hands."

The three children raced for the back door as Flora put away the last of the dishes from Thanksgiving dinner.

Mama untied her apron and hung it on a peg, then smoothed the skirt of her gray dress. "I believe I'll take a walk and get some fresh air while you and the children work on that gingerbread house."

Grandma raised a crooked finger. "If you'll wait a minute, I'll go with you and take a couple of turnovers to Mr. and Mrs. Follo. I know she was feeling poorly this week. She probably didn't get much baking done for Thanksgiving." She quickly wrapped two apple turnovers in a kitchen towel.

Flora longed for fresh air, too, but earlier, at the insistence of her nieces and nephew, she had promised to help them with the gingerbread house. Since Papa, Toby, and Huck had already taken the dogs for a walk, she put the thought of fresh air from her mind and reached for a bowl in which to whip up the icing.

~~~

Sven lit all the lanterns in the shed, wishing their light were brighter, like daylight, but the soft yellow glow would have to do. He reached for a clean rag and began to wipe down the already immaculate finish of the sleigh. His efforts were unnecessary, he knew, but he had to do *something* to ease his nerves while waiting for the others to arrive. Muttering to himself, he rehearsed what he planned to say. In Norwegian, the words would have come a little easier, but English was ever a struggle. Nevertheless, he would rely on Toby's advice and help from the Almighty to speak his piece. It was the best he could do if he wanted to get on with his plans. He prayed that Toby's idea to keep Flora busy at home with the children would work, and that she would not discover this secret meeting with the rest of her kin.

At the sound of voices approaching, Sven's heart lurched. He tossed the rag aside, took a deep breath, put on a smile, and greeted his guests.

"Mrs. Ferguson, Mr. McAdams, Mrs. McAdams, Mr. Harrigan, Toby, good evening!" He patted the dogs, who soon lay quietly on the ground.

When greetings had been returned, Huck, Mrs. McAdams and Mrs. Ferguson wasted no time taking a close look at the sleigh. Mr. McAdams and Toby, who had been faithful to their word, helping every step of the way with the restoration, stood back to watch and listen, smiles on their faces. Mr. Harrigan and the two women wasted no opportunity to issue compliments on every aspect of the work. Sven gave credit where credit was due, naming each person whose effort had made the sleigh like new. Evidently finished with their inspection, Mr. Harrigan and the women approached Sven.

Mrs. McAdams wore a look of wonder. "If I hadn't seen it with my own eyes, I never would have believed how marvelous that old pole cutter looks."

Mrs. Ferguson nodded. "This is the most glorious specimen of a winter conveyance I've ever laid eyes on!"

Mrs. McAdams slid her hand over the curve of the runner. "Anyone in the county would be proud to own this."

Mr. Harrigan's blue eyes gleamed. "Anyone in the *state* would be proud to own it."

Sven smiled. "I hope it is so." His heart pounded. He must speak his piece now, or forfeit the opportunity that he had so carefully planned.

With a look of encouragement from Toby, Sven cleared his throat and began, Norwegian thoughts colliding with their English equivalents.

"Now, I must admit. I have some things besides the sleigh on my mind tonight. Some things I must tell and ask." He swallowed nervously.

Flora's father offered an encouraging smile.

Sven continued. "I speak of Flora. I care very deeply for her." He swallowed again. "I love her." His gaze moved from her father to her mother to her grandmother and to her brother-in-law. Four grins heartened him. He went on. "Now I seek permission to ask Flora for her hand in marriage."

Mrs. McAdams and Mrs. Ferguson exchanged silent nods, then Mr. McAdams replied. "I believe I can speak for all of us when I say you have not only our permission but also our blessing."

A weight heavier than an iron pig lifted from Sven's chest. "One more thing. Please. Say nothing to Flora of what you have seen or heard here. I will reveal all to her when the time is right."

With solemn promises to honor his request, the guests took their leave. Sven sat down on a stool to think. In the time since he had told Flora about his family and his father, he had felt more at peace about the past and confident about the future than ever before. Bowing his head, he thanked God Almighty for His help and His blessing on all that had been accomplished, and that which was yet to come.

CHAPTER 28

Friday afternoon, November 28
The day after Thanksgiving

The doorknocker sounded loudly, sending Pet and Big Boy dashing for the front door, barking fiercely. Flora hurried to the front of the parlor, peeking through the window to discover Dr. Bellows standing on the front stoop. Ignoring the dogs, she grabbed her cloak from the hall tree then hurried out the back door and around to the front.

"Dr. Bellows, what brings you by on this cold and blustery day?" She pulled up her hood against the biting northwest wind and icy snowflakes that had begun to fall.

He turned to her, his gray brows furrowed. "There's trouble down at the cabins. A couple of nasty stray dogs wandered into town today and found some good pickings in the alley, turkey carcasses and such left over from yesterday's dinner. Some children are trying to chase them off and I'm afraid one of them will get badly bit if those dogs aren't removed. I thought of getting help from a couple of furnace men but figured you'd have a kinder approach than they."

"I'll fetch my gloves and see what I can do." A plan forming in her mind, she tossed some of her own family's turkey scraps into each of the two kennels no longer needed by Pet and Big Boy, and shut the gates to keep away scavenging strays. She put on her thick leather work gloves, grabbed two ropes, each about eight feet long, and headed down Stewart Avenue with Dr. Bellows, explaining her plan. "I'll stop by Harris's. If Joseph Marew can part with a couple of meaty leg bones, I ought to be able to convince those strays to follow me home."

A few minutes later, Dr. Bellows helped her to tie a juicy bone securely to one end of each rope. Bait in hand, they headed toward the log cabins. Vicious growls and barks came from behind one of the duplex cabins. Two underfed brindle boxer-like dogs snapped and bared their teeth to protect their supply of turkey and ham bones while a couple of dark-haired boys, about age twelve, taunted them with sticks, attempting to chase them away. A little girl, about age five, clutched a puppy to her soiled, too-small coat, and cried. The moment she saw Dr. Bellows, she came running.

"Doctor, my puppy's bleeding! Look!" She showed him cuts that were clearly the marks of a larger dog's nails.

Dr. Bellows picked up the girl and her dog. "Your puppy will be okay, Annie, I promise. I'm going to take

you inside. You must stay there with your mama while
Miss McAdams and I take these nasty dogs away. Then
I'll come back and fix your puppy's cuts. Okay?"

"Okay."

Flora explained her plan to the boys and asked them
to stand back. Moments later, she and the doctor each
tossed a leg bone to the dogs. The boxers lunged for the
bait. With some tussling and tug-o'-war, they followed
the bones up Stewart Avenue, trailed by the two boys
with sticks. When they reached her back yard, Flora
asked the boys to open the gates to the two kennels and
stand back. Within moments the dogs discovered the turkey scraps, barely noticing their entrapment until the
kennel gates were securely locked.

The boys immediately began to harass the dogs, bang-
ing their sticks against the kennels and poking them
through the slatted sides.

Dr. Bellows grabbed the sticks from their hands,
broke them over his knee, and tossed them aside. Taking
each boy by the collar, he spoke with a sternness Flora
had never heard from the kind doctor before.

"Don't you ever taunt a dog again! Either of you! Understand?"

They nodded.

"You don't want to wind up in my surgery because
some dog you were poking decided to tear you apart, do
you?"

They shook their heads.

Dr. Bellows released the boys. "Now, let's go and see
if we can fix up Annie's puppy, shall we?"

"I'll take care of the puppy, if you'd like," Flora said.

The doctor shook his head. "Thanks for the offer, but you've got your hands full now with those two strays." He started toward town, talking in a grandfatherly fashion with the boys as he went.

Flora turned to the dogs again. The poor creatures were so skinny she could count their ribs. Where had they come from? They were both males, possibly litter mates, and they bore neither collars nor any sign of care from a loving family. From inside the house, Big Boy and Pet barked at the intrusion of two strangers on their territory.

Flora headed inside. Although she had no idea where the dogs were from, she was fairly certain where they could go from here. She warned Mama and Grandma to stay clear of the kennels, then brought her new charges bowls of fresh water. When they had drunk their fill, she headed to the Company Store to leave a message for Mr. Brinks to come see her the next time he was in town. With visions of the two dollars she would receive for the strays, she paused to look over the display case that held the scissors, tweezers, and needle nose pliers she so desperately coveted for her animal care work.

Mr. Powell turned from the candy jars he was restocking and approached. "Is there something I can show you, Miss McAdams?"

She looked up at the sandy-haired man and smiled. "Not until you send Mr. Brinks my way. Then I'll be back with money to spend."

"You may put your purchases on your father's account today, and pay for them later."

Flora shook her head. "I've been warned not to sell the pelt before I've shot the bear. Good day, Mr. Powell."

~~~

Despite Flora's prayers, hopes, and dreams, the afternoon passed by with no sign of Brinks. She helped Mama and Grandma to prepare and serve a supper of turkey dumplings. When the table had been cleared, she fed Pet and Big Boy, then headed to the back yard with bowls of scraps for each of the strays. With the protection of her thick leather work gloves, she managed to set the dishes inside their kennels without getting bit, then stood back to marvel at the urgency with which they consumed their food. She had removed the empty bowls from the kennels and was ready to go inside and leash Pet and Big Boy for a walk when she saw Sven heading her way. The strays bared their teeth and growled as he approach.

He stepped back. "New pets?"

Flora shook her head. "I plan to sell them to Mr. Brinks."

"No!" His expression darkened.

"But these dogs are dangerous, a nuisance in town. They're just what Brinks has been asking for. And he'll pay me a dollar apiece for them."

More agitated than Flora had ever seen him, Sven shook his head and waved his finger. "No! You *must not* sell to Brinks! He will—"

The sound of an explosion cut him off.

Flora drew a sharp breath. "The furnace! Something's gone wrong at—"

The alarm whistle cut her off, warning the entire village of an emergency.

Sven took off at a sprint. Dogs forgotten, Flora lifted her skirt and headed toward the furnace, passed en route by Papa, Toby, and the boarders from Mrs. Lindberg's. As fast as her feet would carry her, she hurried toward the stacks.

At the harbor, men, women, and children were already starting to form a bucket brigade to put out several small fires on the roofs of dockside storage sheds. Flora took her place in line hearing talk that only one man, a laborer, had been injured. As she passed a heavy bucket of water from Charles Mason on her left to George Harris on her right, she caught sight of Dr. Bellows in the distance, tending a man sitting on the ground. Silently, she prayed for God's healing hand on the suffering man and His help in putting out the fires. A few minutes later, word came down the line that the laborer wasn't badly hurt.

Flora breathed a sigh. "Thank God for that!"

"And thank God the fires will soon be out, too, by the looks of it," said Charles.

George nodded. "All will be back to normal with a few roof repairs."

Within minutes the bucket brigade disbanded. Flora started for home, coming across Frank Brinks aboard his wagon outside Harris's market.

"Mr. Brinks, you're just the man I've been looking for. I've got two dogs for you!"

He raised a scruffy brow. "Scrappy ones?"

"Yes, sir. Guaranteed!"

"Climb aboard. I'll drive you home."

Flora shook her head. "I'll walk. I'll see you up at my house in five minutes."

Sure enough, by the time she had gathered together the food scraps needed as lures, and the ropes to keep the dogs under control, Brinks had pulled up front.

His appearance in the back yard set off the two strays in the kennels, and Pet and Big Boy inside the house.

The snarling and growling put a nefarious smile on Brinks' lips. He reached into his pocket and held up two silver dollars. "These are yours, soon as you get those mutts aboard my wagon."

"Yes, sir. I'll need a little time. And it would be best if you pull your wagon ahead, out of sight, and sit there, still and quiet."

He nodded.

With Brinks out of view and food for rewards, Flora soon had the attention of the strays. One dog at a time, using soft-spoken words and nibbles of meat, she put leashes around their necks and moved them onto the bed of the wagon where she tied them securely.

Brinks handed her the silver dollars. "Much obliged, Miss McAdams. Let me know if you find another pair like these."

She nodded. "I'm wondering. How are the first two dogs getting along?"

He started to pull away. "Snarly as ever. Good night!"

She headed for the back door, eager to take Pet and Big Boy on their evening walk. Leashes in hand, she led them down Stewart Avenue hoping to catch sight of Sven, but he was not among other boarders returning to Mrs. Lindberg's, nor did she see him amongst the fellows lingering outside the furnace to recount the evening's events and reminisce over disasters of the past.

Continuing up Sheldon Avenue, she headed for Cedar Lane and circled back to the house, hoping to encounter Sven there. When he was not in sight, she assumed that he had gone to work on the sleigh.

Thoughts of the completed restoration put a smile on her face. Toby had already told her that the old pole cutter was too fine for words. In two days, Sven would finally let her see it, and she could hardly wait.

But tomorrow, she would take the two dollars from Mr. Brinks and spend it on much needed supplies at the Company Store.

CHAPTER 29

Flora gazed with satisfaction at the assortment of supplies on the counter of the Company Store. Powers and Weightman Sulphate of Morphine, round tip scissors, tweezers, needle-nose pliers, a large needle, a spool of heavy weight thread, a large tooth comb, and a stiff brush.

Mr. Powell ran a hand through his light brown hair as he ciphered the sum on a piece of brown paper. "That comes to a grand total of two dollars and forty-nine cents, Miss McAdams."

"Two dollars and forty-nine cents?" How could that be?

He reviewed the price of each item and added again with the same results. Flora set aside the scissors and handed him the two silver dollars she had received from Brinks.

Mr. Powell tossed the coins into his cash box and offered her a smile and a penny. "Your change, Miss McAdams, and thank you for your patronage."

She was about to drop the penny into her pocket when she caught sight of a jar containing her favorite candy. She slid the coin across the counter to Mr. Powell, helped herself to a horehound drop, placed her purchases into her basket, and stepped out of the door. A biting northwest wind whipped at her cape and hood. She pulled them tighter and headed for home with a whispered prayer of thanks for the much-needed supplies. But the words had barely passed from her lips when she began a mental list of the items that she had *not* been able to buy with the money from Brinks. Scissors, hydrogen peroxide, and cotton batten. These she would purchase as soon as she had sold enough raffle tickets on the sleigh.

Her spirits took flight. Tomorrow after supper, Sven would finally let her see it. As her feet crunched against limestone and slag pebbles, she gazed up at the dark gray clouds. Would the cold wind bring snow? Thus far, little had fallen and the ground was bare. Visions came to mind of a thick white blanket covering the road and a magnificent black sleigh with gracefully curved runners dashing through town behind a pair of swift chestnut horses. How attractive the sleigh would look on display outside the Machine Shop where anyone coming to town would see it and want to buy a ticket on it. But she wouldn't leave that to chance. She would go out herself on Monday morning from business to business and house to house selling tickets.

But first she must tend to the business of today. Pet and Big Boy waited for their walk, and Mama and Grandma had already reminded her of their need for help with the Saturday cleaning and cooking chores. As soon as she stepped into the house she put away her purchases, then set out with the dogs on a walk around Cedar Lane. Home again, she headed upstairs. When the bedrooms had been set in order and swept and dusted, she went downstairs to help Mama do the same in the parlor and dining room.

In the afternoon, she helped Mama to clean out and peel a pumpkin for pies and Grandma to pare potatoes and carrots and chop onions and celery for the beef stew she was planning for supper. With the pumpkin and stew simmering under the watchful eyes of Mama and Grandma, Flora tucked a clean cotton rag and a near-empty bottle of hydrogen peroxide into a satchel and headed to town to check on Annie's puppy. As the Machine Shop came into view, she prayed that this evening would be a quiet one and that Sven would accompany her on their evening dog walk. She had started down the log cabin alley where Annie lived when a familiar voice called her name. She turned to find Huck beckoning to her from his wagon. She hurried to greet him.

"Huck, what brings you to town? And without Lavinia and the children?"

"Dan and Rose have been down with the flu and it looks like Violet is catching it, too. So many have fallen ill in Sac Bay, there's not a drop of medicine left in that town so Lavinia sent me here to fetch some. She asked me to extend our regrets that we won't be here for the unveiling of the sleigh tomorrow. Be sure and tell your folks. I won't take the time to stop by there myself. Lavinia needs me home as quickly as I can get there."

"Sorry about the children. I'll tell Mama and Papa. Give our love to everyone at home. I hope the little ones recover soon."

"As do I." Huck set his wagon in motion again.

~~~

The last remnants of daylight were fading fast when Flora spooned stew leftovers into bowls and offered them to Pet and Big Boy. While they eagerly devoured her offerings, Flora reflected on her visit to Annie, thankful that the puppy was recovering without infection. She was thankful, too, that he appeared to be well-fed and loved, and that Annie's mother had agreed to allow Flora to perform the surgery that would prevent him from fathering puppies as soon as he was old enough.

She set Pet's and Big Boy's empty bowls aside, leashed the dogs, and headed out the back door, smiling at the sight of Sven in conversation with Papa and Toby, who had gone out after supper to split wood. Her smile faded as Papa, grim-faced, turned to her.

"I'm afraid Sven has some bad news about those dogs you sold to Brinks last night."

Flora gazed into his blue-gray eyes. "Are they dead?"

He shook his head. "They are alive, but only for a while. Brinks will make them fight each other, same as the last two you sold him."

"He turns the dogs against each other," said Toby. "He takes bets on them and makes lots of money for himself. Then he puts them in a pit and they fight until one is dead, and the other is so bad off, he dies soon after."

Flora's blood ran hot. "I thought Brinks used the dogs to guard his place. When I asked how the last two dogs were getting along, he said, 'Snarly as ever.'"

Sven shook his head. "He lied."

Flora's stomach soured. "I wanted to save their lives. Instead, I sold them to a future of cruel suffering and . . ." She shuddered. "Good glory, I can't believe I have done such a horrible thing!"

Papa placed his hand on her shoulder. "You couldn't have known."

Toby set aside his maul. "It was a well-guarded secret."

"I only learned of it recently," said Sven. "Last night, when I saw the two dogs," he nodded toward the empty kennels, "I started to tell you, but the explosion . . . "

Sven had been expressing his adamant disapproval of her plan to sell to Brinks, and the explosion and alarm had cut him off. Now, she had taken the dreadful man's money for two more dogs. But they were evidently still alive.

Flora gazed down at Pet and Big Boy. "I'm going to put these fellows inside, then I'm going out to Brinks' place and get those two dogs back."

Sven followed after her. "You cannot. It is too dangerous."

"I don't care. I'm going to do what's right!" With her own dogs inside, she removed their leashes to take with her, tucked several cheese cubes into her pockets, pulled on her leather work gloves, and headed out the back door again.

Sven caught her firmly by the arm. "Do not go to Brinks. I beg you."

She yanked free and faced him, her jaw set. "Go with me, or stay here, but *don't* try to stop me." She headed for the street at a fast clip.

Sven kept a silent pace alongside her.

Within moments, Papa and Toby caught up, rifles and lanterns in tow.

Nearing the hotel, Flora barely noticed George Harris and Charles Mason on the porch until George called out.

"Toby, where you headed in such a hurry?"

"To Brinks' saloon to put his dog fighting out of business. Come with us. I'll take you on in a game of pool when we get back."

"It's a deal!" George hopped over the porch rail to join them, followed by Charles.

Farther along, Mr. Grennell, Joseph Marew, Mr. Ferris, and John Chaulklin each picked up his rifle and lantern and joined the mission.

On the long walk to the saloon, flanked by Sven on one side and Papa on the other, Flora silently prayed for a safe and successful rescue of the two dogs. Suddenly a new worry emerged.

"Papa, I've already spent the two dollars Mr. Brinks gave me for the dogs. Surely he'll ask for his money back. What shall I do?"

"Put your trust in God. He'll supply."

Flora prayed again. Nevertheless, the closer they got to the saloon, the tighter the knot grew in her stomach.

Soon, they could see dim lights from the windows of Brinks' establishment.

Coming from behind the tavern were the pitiful whines and howls of the dogs she had sold him yesterday. They played a soulful descant to the happy voices leaking from within. Laborers with cash from yesterday's monthly payday were eagerly squandering their meager earnings on liquid bliss and cruel sport.

Sven marched up to the door, slammed it open and stepped in, shoulders square, chest broad. Flora followed close behind him. Smoke filled the air and the stench of cigars nearly sent her into a coughing fit.

Some of the revelers turned to look. Several others were too drunk to notice them. Brinks stood behind the bar where he was pouring another whiskey for some drunken soul. By the time he looked up, Papa, Toby, and the others had crowded in behind them.

Brinks grinned and raised his whiskey bottle. "Can I pour you fellas—and lady—a drink?"

Flora stepped forward, heart pounding, and spoke loud and clear. "I didn't come here to drink. I came to take back the two dogs I sold you."

He slammed the bottle down so hard it almost broke. "You can't do that! I bought 'em, fair and square!" He glared at her, his cheeks flushed.

"I'm canceling the deal. I won't have you putting them to a cruel death in dog fights!"

He reached beneath the counter, raised a rifle to his shoulder, and pointed it straight at her. "Get out of here! Go back where you came from, before I do ya harm. And don't you dare go near those dogs!"

Flora's knees grew so weak they almost buckled. From the corner of her eye, she caught a glimpse of Papa, Toby, and others raising their rifles to point them at Brinks.

CHAPTER 30

Papa issued a calm warning. "Put your gun down, Brinks. No point getting shot over a couple of dogs now, is there?"

Evidently seeing the odds against him, Brinks began to lower his rifle.

"That's it," said Papa, "set the rifle gently on the counter and step back."

When he had complied, George Harris moved up to the counter and took the rifle in hand. "Hey! This is *my* rifle! You stole this out of my back room!"

Brinks shook his head. "You're mistaken!"

George let out a hoot and pointed to the stock. "Mistaken about my very own initials that I carved on it?"

A customer guffawed. "He's got you there, Brinks!"

"Flora, Sven, Toby, go and get the dogs." Papa's nodded in the direction of the whines and howls.

Brinks stamped his boot. "What about that two dollars I paid? I'll turn you three into the sheriff for stealing my dogs. I got plenty of witnesses to back up my claim!"

George Harris stared him in the face. "You'll turn them in, will you? Are you sure you want to do that?"

Charles Mason stepped forward with a friendly smile. "Mr. Brinks, sir, I'm willing to guess that if you'll forget all about those dogs and the two dollars you paid, Mr. Harris, here, just might forget to tell the sheriff he found his gun in your possession."

Brinks' customers hooted and howled. Much relieved, Flora turned to go, Sven and Toby with her. Out back, she warned the men to keep their distance, then she approached the caged dogs slowly, speaking in a soft voice. Quickly they accepted the cheese cubes she offered, and shortly after, allowed her to leash them and lead them from their cages without a single growl. She was ready to head for home when she saw that Toby had discovered a door ajar at the back of the saloon.

Raising his lantern, he opened the door. "Pig iron and polecats! Sven, look here!"

Flora stood at a distance with the dogs while the two investigated. Moments later, they emerged, arms loaded with clothing. They set the apparel on the ground in two heaps and while Toby held the lantern, Sven began going through it.

Papa and the others, done inside, came around back to discover the find, their lanterns shedding additional light on the purloined garments.

George Harris held up a pair of trousers. "These belong to my father. He bought them new, and they were stolen before he even got to wear them!"

John Chaulklin found his overcoat. "I'm mighty glad to meet up with this again."

Mr. Ferris claimed a shirt. "I wondered where this had got to."

Mr. Grinnell held up a vest. "This here's mine, all right. Been missing it for a month and now I know why."

Joseph Marew dangled a pair of suspenders. "I'd know these anywhere."

Toby began to straighten up the mess of unclaimed items. "Seems we've discovered the identity of the clothing thief who's been pillaging the town these past two months."

"Sure enough," said Papa. "I thought we were done here, but I can see we've got a little more business to do inside with Mr. Brinks."

Papa led Sven and Toby, who carried the remains of the backroom discovery, into the tavern. The others followed, all but Charles Mason who stood several yards from Flora.

Charles pulled out his handkerchief to mop his brow and blow his nose. When he headed toward Flora, the dogs bared their teeth and growled, stopping him in his tracks.

"You'd better not come any closer, Mr. Mason. These fellows aren't in any mood to make friends, unless you're armed with plenty of cheese cubes."

"So that's your secret."

At the sound of his voice, the dogs barked and growled. Another cheese cube apiece distracted and quieted them. They remained calm until voices from inside the saloon swelled to a roar. Nervously, they emitted low growls. Flora led them a little way down the dark road toward home and paused there to wait for the others. A minute later, the men poured out of the tavern, full of talk and laughter, and relieved of the purloined apparel.

"Brinks sure knows how to make himself a town full of enemies," said George Harris.

"I wonder how many customers he'll have, now that they know he's been stealing from them," said Toby.

"He should have thought of that before he decided to help himself to their duds," said Papa.

The approach of Sven, Toby, and Papa put both dogs on guard. Flora had a hard time keeping her grip on the leashes.

"Go on ahead, fellows." Flora wrapped the leashes around her hands more securely. "I'll be a few paces behind you with the dogs."

George Harris and the others brought up the rear. They had walked about an eighth of a mile when George shouted.

"Hey, everybody! Look behind you!"

Flora looked over her shoulder. Flames licked at the roof of the tavern.

"Those customers must have been a little angrier than I thought," said Papa. "We'd better go back and make sure everyone got out. Mason, stay with Flora."

The others took off at a trot. They returned a few minutes later.

"No one hurt," said Papa, "but they're madder than hornets. They ran Brinks off with nothing but the clothes on his back."

"What is your saying?" asked Sven. "All is well that ends well?"

As laughter carried them toward town, Flora thanked God that she and everyone with her were headed home in safety, and that she had been able to rescue the dogs. But her heart was heavy for the first two dogs she had sold to Brinks. She asked God's forgiveness for the greed that had clouded her judgement and enticed her to do business with the unsavory character. And she prayed for help in training and caring for these two new dogs that had come into her possession.

A quarter of an hour later, they arrived back in town. Mr. Ferris, Mr. Grinnell, and Joseph Marew went their way. Toby and George headed for a shoot-out at the pool table. Charles turned in at the hotel to take hot tea, honey, and lemon for the sniffles that were coming on.

Home again, Papa left his lantern with Sven and went inside to tell Mama and Grandma all that had happened.

In the back yard, Sven waited while Flora secured the dogs behind the gates of their kennels, brought them food and water, then leashed Pet and Big Boy for their belated evening walk. How excited they were, nearly pulling Flora off her feet in their hurry to head down Stewart Avenue and leave their scent at their favorite stopping places along the way.

Sven grabbed hold of the leashes and handed Flora the lantern. With the dogs under control, he placed an arm about Flora's waist and they continued at a moderate pace.

Although Flora customarily did the talking on the nightly strolls, her mind was too preoccupied to initiate conversation, and her heart remained heavy for the dogs that had met a cruel demise behind Brinks' tavern. Quietly, she and Sven followed the dogs up Sheldon Avenue, and circled Cedar Lane. Flora was thankful for the thick growth of trees that sheltered them from the stiff wind that began gusting in off the lake and driving icy snowflakes horizontally. When they returned home, they stopped near the front stoop, out of sight of the two dogs in back to prevent another outburst of their barking and growling.

Flora set the lantern on the front step.

When Pet and Big Boy settled at her feet, Sven dropped their leashes and tipped Flora's face toward him. "You are quiet. *Too* quiet."

A tear leaked from her eye and ran down the side of her face. "I can't stop thinking . . . about the first dogs I sold to Brinks. Good glory, I feel so guilty."

"You couldn't know," Sven's quiet words bathed her in tenderness. "Only his customers knew. I learned of it two days ago from one of them." He brushed the tear from her face, then wrapped his arms about her and pulled her tightly to him.

Flora shook with silent sobs and let her tears flow, comforted by Sven's caring arms and the closeness of Pet and Big Boy who pressed firmly against her and Sven, determined to be included in the hug.

Sven released her, wiped her face dry with his handkerchief, then took her by the shoulders and gazed straight into her eyes.

"Do not feel guilty. You saved these two dogs. And tonight you saved two more." He nodded toward the back yard. "For this, you can be happy. And remember. Tomorrow you will see the sleigh!"

With that, he left her—not to return next door to Mrs. Lindberg's, but to disappear down Stewart Avenue.

Flora had no doubt he was headed for the sleigh. She could hardly wait to see the wonderful winter conveyance that he had worked so hard on all these many weeks. Tomorrow could not possibly come soon enough.

CHAPTER 31

The five o'clock whistle had not yet faded to silence as Sven pulled off his soiled flannel work shirt and put on his good white cotton shirt. He donned his sack coat, brown winter jacket, and plush hat, headed out the door of the Machine Shop, and took a path straight toward the snow-covered shed alongside the sawmill. The sight of Mr. Ferris and the pair of chestnut mares from the stock barn made him smile. Joseph Marew and Maggie Coughlin were there, too, helping to make the restored sleigh ready for its maiden run. Within moments, Toby, his papa, Mr. Grennell, and others who had worked on the sleigh from time to time joined them, eager to witness the first run of the like-new cutter.

Mr. Ferris checked the hitch one last time. "She's ready to go."

Sven nodded and stepped up into the cutter.

Maggie stepped forward. "You'll find bear robes and foot warmers in each seat. Don't forget—you owe Joseph and me a ride after Flora's kin have had their turn."

"I won't forget." Sven rested his feet on the foot warmer and pulled the bear robe over his lap. "Thank you. Thank you all!"

With one last nod, Sven slapped the reins, issued a command, and the horses lunged forward, pulling the sleigh out of the shed and across the snowy road toward Sac Bay. After a couple of minutes, satisfied that the horses, hitch, and sleigh were safe and in proper working order, he turned back toward town, eager to see the look on Flora's face when he pulled up.

~~~

The instructions Sven had given Flora when he stopped by briefly after the midday meal had been very clear. She was to dress in her warmest cloak, boots, mittens, and scarf and stand on the front stoop at ten minutes past five.

At nine minutes past, wrapped warm enough to withstand a blizzard, she headed out the front door. A thick blanket of snow covered the ground that had been bare last night, and she thanked God for the beauty of the winter mantel that had fallen over the village and laid down the perfect surface for running a sleigh. She gazed down Stewart Avenue. No sleigh was in sight, but Papa and Toby, bundled in scarves and stocking caps, were headed for home. Mama and Grandma, dressed in warm winter coats, emerged from the front door and stood close to her on either side. At the edge of the front yard,

Papa and Toby stepped off the road and looked back toward town.

The faint tinkling of sleigh bells jingled in the cold, crisp air.

Mama's face lit with excitement. "He's coming, Flora!"

A pair of chestnut horses pranced up the street. The ground vibrated. Flora's heart pounded to the rhythm of the horses' feet. They came to a halt directly in front of the house. The sleigh carrying Sven was so magnificent, Flora's jaw went slack. She searched futilely for words.

Sven, clad in his brown plush hat and thick brown jacket, beamed at her from the front seat.

Mama nudged Flora. "What do you think?"

Grandma rested her hand on Flora's arm. "Isn't that just about the most beautiful thing you've ever seen in all your born days?"

"What's the matter, Flora?" Papa asked. "Cat got your tongue?"

Toby playfully punched her shoulder. "Say *something,* Flora."

She struggled to set her tongue in motion. "Good glory! It's *red!"*

Laughter rang in the air.

Mama squeezed her waist. "We can see that, dear."

Flora struggled to explain. "I . . . I was expecting it to be black like it was before. But it's *red!* A *beautiful bright red!"* She flew off the porch to take a good look.

Sven stepped down, following her closely as she scrutinized every detail.

The glossy red body, painted smooth as glass, had been trimmed with white stripes that followed the graceful curves of the dash. The runners also wore a new coat of red paint. And the front and rear seats sported brand new red woolen upholstery over thick padding.

Flora removed her mitten to run her hand over the smooth red body. She sank her fingers into the plush upholstery. How much time, effort, and skill had been required to transform the neglected, broken-down cutter into this bright, beautiful sleigh? With a heart full of gratitude, she turned to Sven, pushing words past the lump in her throat.

"It's beautiful . . . more beautiful than I imagined. How can I thank you?" She rose on her toes and planted a quick kiss on his cheek.

Color rose all the way to his forehead and a smile spread across his mouth. "Your words and your kiss are thanks enough. Now get in. You must take a ride." He helped her into the sleigh and took a seat close beside her, arranging the bear robe over their laps.

With a slap of the reins, the sleigh jerked forward. Rounding the turn to Harbor Street, he set course up Furnace Hill, past the school, then put the horses in a gallop toward the northeast. Cold wind whipped at Flora's scarf and stung her face as the sleigh glided swiftly over the snowy landscape. The speed and exhilaration set her pulse pounding and sent her into joyous laughter. Past the charred remains of the old tavern they flew, circling around and returning home.

With Mama, Papa, and Grandma tucked snuggly into the rear seat, they set out for a short tour of the town. Joseph Marew, Maggie Coughlin, Mr. Grennell, Marian Phillips, Mr. Ferris, the elder and younger Harrises, Dr. and Mrs. Bellows, and several others of Flora's acquaintance stood along the street to wave and extend their compliments on the fine looking rig. Home again, Toby and Elin occupied the back seat for another flying tour past the former tavern.

When they entered the village, Sven let them out in front of the hotel. Then he reached into his pocket and handed Flora the stack of raffle tickets he'd had printed. Two passengers at a time, he invited all those who had helped fix the sleigh to take the back seat for a ride around Cedar Lane. Joseph and Maggie were first. Flora learned that Joseph had helped paint the sleigh red, and Maggie had put her seamstress skills to the task of reupholstering the seats. They were followed by Mr. Hines, boss at the sawmill who had donated lumber and loaned one of his sheds for a workplace, and Mr. Grennell, who had skillfully repaired the floorboards. After them came Mr. Cumberland and John Meehan, who had worked on the runners, and Thomas Young who had put his hand to painting the narrow white lines of trim. When they had stepped out, Mr. Ferris, who had loaned the team and hitched them up, and Mr. Powell who had obtained the upholstery fabric at a sharply reduced price, occupied the back seat.

They were followed by George Harris, who had helped sand the new floorboards, and his wife, Clara; Joseph Harris who had donated the paint, and his wife, Harriet; Dr. and Mrs. Bellows, who had contributed the money for the red woolen fabric; Henry Pinchin who had sanded the body, and his intended, Mary Caffey, and many others who had had no part in fixing the sleigh but were fascinated by its dashing appearance. Everyone who took a ride also bought tickets and was instructed to fill out the stub with his or her name and address and deposit it into the keg on the hotel porch. The keg had been fitted out with a slot and a padlocked door for the drawing.

Dr. Bellows bought the largest number of tickets—ten for himself and ten for his wife. Flora's pockets were bulging with coins by the time Sven returned to the hotel with the last of the passengers, Big Toby and Jane Bigelow. They were eager to buy one ticket apiece, then return to the work waiting for them inside the hotel.

Mr. Ferris, Mr. Follo, and others stood on the porch, still abuzz about the astounding transformation of the old abandoned cutter. But why hadn't Flora seen any sign of Charles Mason, either at church this morning or this evening amongst the sleigh enthusiasts? Perhaps he was nursing his cold.

Sven hopped down and offered a hand to assist Flora.

She stared at him in confusion. "Shouldn't you take me home? It's way past suppertime."

He grinned. "No supper for you tonight. Instead, I take you to *dinner* at the hotel."

"But—"

Mr. Ferris cut her off. "That's right, Miss Flora. Sven has it all planned. While you two are inside, Mr. Follo and I will take the sleigh and keg to the Machine Shop. When folks come into town and want to buy tickets on it, Sven will be right handy to sell to 'em." Mr. Follo lifted the keg to his shoulder and stepped off the porch, followed by Mr. Ferris, who stepped up into the sleigh. He gestured to Flora to accept the hand Sven had extended to help her down.

Flora was about to protest the cost of dinner at the hotel when Sven placed his hands about her waist, picked her up off the seat, and set her gently on the ground.

The elder Mr. Harris, manager of the hotel, beckoned from the porch. "Mr. Jorgensen, Miss McAdams, your table is ready, and your dinner is waiting."

CHAPTER 32

Mr. Harris held the door open and led them into the dining room to a small, round table for two in the corner by the front window, nicely secluded from a few others dining at the opposite end of the room.

Big Toby appeared in an instant, his smile reaching all the way to his blue eyes. "I'll take your wraps for ya, and Jane will bring ya the appetizer."

Flora nodded and took in her surroundings. The white damask tablecloth, polished silverware, gleaming crystal, and napkins cleverly folded to stand erect, spoke of the new elegance Joseph Harris had brought to the hotel during its renovation this fall. She unfolded the napkin and laid it across her lap. Jane appeared with cups of hot chowder and a pitcher of ice water to fill their goblets.

Flora tasted the soup, far richer and thicker than any ever served at home. She was savoring its creamy flavor when she noticed the table centerpiece. On a fancy lace doily was a tiny carving of the magnificent red sleigh. It was trimmed with a white stripe, upholstered in red wool, and fitted out with little metal runners curved exactly like the real ones. Flora drew a quick breath as she picked it up and held it in the palm of her hand. Its dainty size and its unerring likeness to the restored sleigh in every detail fascinated her.

When her gaze met Sven's, he answered her unasked question. "Three weeks ago I asked your brother-in-law to make a memento for you of this night." He turned it over and showed her Huck's initials on the bottom side. "I hoped he and his family could come tonight. He brought this to me yesterday with news that the children are sick."

Flora nodded. With a silent prayer of thanks for Huck's special gift, and a petition for the recovery of his children, she set the sleigh on its doily and gazed into Sven's eyes. They appeared more blue than gray in the soft light of the small table lamp, and she read there his unspoken thoughts.

I have planned this night for you, to bring you happiness. And though my words are few, my actions are many. When you are happy, I am happy.

She wanted to scold him for spending his hard-earned money on a meal at the hotel when they could have eaten frugally at home, but to do so would be the height of ungratefulness. Emotion welled up inside—appreciation for Sven's hard work and for his many hours of devotion to a difficult task. More importantly, she now realized how, in the process of turning a decrepit cast-off into a coveted conveyance, he had also managed to transform Fayette into a community with a spirit of cooperation and an accomplishment of mutual pride.

Silently, she thanked God for Sven's success with the sleigh, and for his meticulous planning of this special evening, right down to the centerpiece on the table. A lump gathered in her throat, causing her to set her soup spoon aside.

Sven lifted a spoonful of soup to his mouth and sipped it. "Almost as good as my mother's. But you do not like the soup?"

Flora shook her head and took up her spoon again, forcing the lump from her throat. "I like it very much. I'm just . . ." She searched for words, but this was not the time to tell him that a freshet of feelings had hindered her hunger. Leaving her sentence unfinished, she dipped into the soup, managing to focus on its creaminess once more, the bits of delicately flavored bass renewing her appetite.

Outside the window, in the lamplight spilling from the porch, delightful flakes of frozen lace wafted down from dark heavens to spread a new layer of white on white. There was no place on earth that she would rather be than right here, right now, with this man of unfathomable depths and unpredictable surprises.

Sven finished the last of his soup and set down his spoon. "Are you not feeling well? You are quiet tonight."

"I am well, but I am overwhelmed."

His brow wrinkled.

She swallowed the last of her soup and attempted to explain. "I knew the sleigh would be wonderful. I even had a picture of it in my mind, all black and beautiful, the seats recovered, the runners repaired." She paused to reflect on the inaccurate image that she had carried in her mind for two-and-a-half months.

Jane came to take away the empty soup cups and spoons and place before them plates of rare roast beef accompanied by peas, pearl onions, and small potatoes garnished with butter and parsley. A marvelous aroma wafted up. Flora took fork and knife in hand, eager for a taste.

Sven cut into the meat. His gaze lifted to Flora. "You do not like red paint on the sleigh?" He popped a morsel of beef into his mouth.

"Good glory, I *love* red! And for the sleigh, it is so much better than the black I had imagined." She took another bite of beef, savoring its juiciness while pondering all that had occurred since her first glimpse of Sven and the sleigh. It was almost too much to comprehend.

Sven set knife and fork aside. "Flora?"

Her name was almost a whisper. She gazed up at him, the dim lamplight flickering against a worry line in his forehead. She swallowed the melt-in-your-mouth beef.

"Yes, Sven?"

"I must ask a question. And you must tell the truth."

What question could possibly be the cause of his worry on a night as wonderful as this?

"Are you happy?"

"Oh, Sven, I am much *more* than happy." Flora reached across the table and took his hand in hers. "Tonight, I am thrilled, awed, overwhelmed, astonished, amazed and benumbed by the sleigh, this dinner, and . . ." She paused and simply gazed into the eyes of the most remarkable man she had ever known.

Sven squeezed her fingers. "And?"

"And you."

Color invaded Sven's cheeks as a smile spread across his face. Taking both of her hands in his, he leaned closer. "There is something I must tell you."

Flora sensed the sudden seriousness of his tone and with baited breath, whispered, "Yes, Sven?"

"Jeg er—sorry. Norwegian fights with English." He shook his head as if clearing it of his mother tongue.

"Jeg er? What does that mean?"

"I am," Sven replied. "It is your first lesson in Norwegian. But I did not intend to teach Norwegian tonight." He grew silent.

Flora couldn't contain her curiosity. "You were going to tell me something about yourself? 'I am . . .'?"

"I am very fond of you."

"And I am very fond of *you.*"

Sven continued. "We have been a little while friends. But my care for you . . . it is not little. It is wide, wider than the ocean I crossed."

Though Sven had chosen unusual words, Flora understood their meaning. His profession of love thrilled her clear through. She couched her own words carefully. "I care for you deeply, too, Sven. I don't suppose there's an ocean wide enough or deep enough to contain what I am feeling right now."

He gave a slight nod. "When I think of the future, you are there. I cannot think of it without you."

"Nor can I imagine my life without you." A moment lapsed in which Flora simply basked in the significance of their admissions, broken by the appearance of Jane.

"Is everything all right? You two haven't eaten much. Is the meat too rare? I can have it cooked longer."

Sven released Flora's hands and turned to Jane with a smile. "My meat is fine, thank you."

Flora managed a smile of her own. "And so is mine. Everything is excellent. And I intend to eat every bite." She wanted to tell Jane that it wasn't the meat, but the *moment* that was rare. Instead, she pushed those thoughts aside to take fork and knife in hand and cut another piece of the tasty beef.

Conversation seemed unnecessary as they continued their main course, their silence broken occasionally by a question or comment that came to Flora's mind about the restoration of the sleigh or her plans for the money it was generating. When they had finished their main course, Jane appeared again.

"May I bring you dessert?"

Sven nodded.

Jane picked up their plates and headed for the kitchen, returning with ice water to refill their goblets. Flora gave Sven a puzzled look. "Shouldn't she have offered us some choices or told us what kinds of pie were available?"

Sven's blue eyes twinkled. "Not tonight. You will see. The best is yet to come."

A few minutes later Jane brought teacups and a pot of freshly brewed tea. Then she set up a serving stand next to their table. "I'll be right out with your dessert, Mr. Jorgensen."

He nodded, and she disappeared into the kitchen once more.

Flora sipped her tea. What dessert could possibly surpass the marvels of the evening thus far?

CHAPTER 33

Flora glanced frequently in the direction of the kitchen, so eager to see the dessert that a minute of waiting seemed like an hour. But soon the door swung open and Jane emerged carrying a silver tray bearing a red and white dessert. When she set it on the stand beside the table, Flora realized it was a confectioner's rendering of the sleigh on snow in the form of frosted cake, and in the front seat sat a marzipan woman and man bearing a remarkable resemblance to her and Sven.

Jane lifted a knife to cut a piece, but Flora put her palm out. "Let me just look at it for a minute." She glanced up at Sven. "Good glory! I can't believe how well this matches the cutter, right down to the thin white trim line!" She focused again on the sleigh. "And look at the people on the seat. She's wearing a cloak identical to mine, and he has a brown jacket and hat like yours. This is so clever, I hate to spoil it by cutting into it."

"You do not want a taste?" Sven asked.

Flora pointed to a corner of the bottom layer, a rectangle covered in fluffy white frosting topped with finely shredded coconut. "Cut our pieces from there, please, Jane. I can't bear to have you cut into the sleigh just yet."

Jane did as Flora asked, serving two pieces of chocolate cake topped by white frosting and coconut.

Sven picked up his fork, and held it poised over the chocolate cake. "The baker even remembered the dirt."

Flora laughed. "Hopefully, he forgot about the stones that are everywhere in the soil at Fayette." Putting a forkful into her mouth, she immediately bit into a nut.

Sven must have done the same, for he grinned and shook his head. "I fear you are wrong. The 'stones' are here, too."

"In the form of broken walnuts, thank goodness." Flora savored the richness of the nutty chocolate cake and creamy coconut frosting as she continued to study the confectionery sleigh, still awed by the accuracy and resourcefulness it reflected. Finishing her last bite, she set down her fork and smiled at Sven. "This dessert—this whole dinner—has been truly amazing. Thank you."

"Would you like more cake?"

She shook her head. "I've had way more than I needed already, but everything was so delicious, I just had to clean my plate."

Joseph Harris approached their table. "How was everything tonight, folks?"

Flora offered a wide smile. "Excellent, Mr. Harris. The soup, the roast beef, the cake, I don't see how they could have been any better."

"Good! That's what I like to hear from my customers." He turned to Sven. "Is there anything else, Mr. Jorgensen?" Sven shook his head. "We are finished."

Mr. Harris nodded. "Jane will box the cake for you, and I'll have Big Toby bring your wraps."

Sven shoved coins beneath his plate, then helped Flora into her cloak. He handed her the carved sleigh from Huck, then pulled on his jacket while Jane boxed the cake. He tucked the confection safely under his arm and ushered Flora out of the hotel.

Her feet wanted to race up Stewart Avenue. "I can't wait until Mama and Grandma get a look at that cake. Is it all right if they have some with their tea tonight?"

Sven grinned. "I hope they will."

"This whole evening has been so incredible." Flora's words flowed fast as the newly rebuilt cutter. "I still can't believe it. The sleigh is too wonderful for words! And from the number of tickets we've sold, everyone else thinks so, too." She jingled the coins in her pockets. "Dinner at the hotel came as such a surprise. You shouldn't have done it, but I'm glad you did! And the memento from Huck and the cake . . . how can I possibly thank you for it all?" They reached the front stoop, dimly lit by the light spilling from the parlor window, and she gazed up at Sven. "Are you coming inside?"

He shook his head and handed her the box. "Tomorrow comes early." Taking her gently by the shoulders, he bent to place a kiss on her cheek, then took off quickly for his boarding house next door.

Flora watched him go, the gentleness of his kiss still fresh on her cheek, and a myriad of unspoken feelings welling up in her heart.

~~~

3:30 A.M. the following morning
Monday, December 1

Loud, urgent knocks on the front door sent Pet and Big Boy racing downstairs, barking furiously, and rousing Flora from a sound sleep and pleasant dreams of her dinner with Sven. In the next bedroom, Toby grumbled, "Who could that be at this time of night?"

Downstairs, Papa issued stern commands to quiet the dogs. Then, the voice of Dr. Bellows floated up to Flora as he renewed his acquaintance with Pet and Big Boy then addressed Papa.

"So sorry to wake you at this hour, Angus. You know I wouldn't have come if it weren't an emergency. I've got a favor to ask."

"Come in, Doc."

Flora pulled on her robe and dashed barefoot down the cold stairs, reaching the front entrance at the same time as Mama and Grandma.

The gray-bearded doctor's gaze encompassed them all. "Four laborers are in a bad way with the flu. So bad I've moved them to my place so Mrs. Bellows and I can tend them more conveniently. Now, Charlie Mason's taken ill. But my place is full up. Can't take another patient. And I know if Charlie stays where he is, he won't get the care he needs, not to mention that he could infect others. Joe Harris doesn't have the extra help at the hotel to nurse Charlie night and day."

"I'll do it," said Mama. "Mr. Mason can bed down on the sofa in the front parlor. We'll make the room into an infirmary." She turned to Papa. "Is that all right with you?"

Papa nodded.

Toby, still wiping sleep from his eyes, joined the others and was quickly told of the plan.

Dr. Bellows turned to Mama. "There's one thing more. Charlie insisted that I ask if you would take over his teaching duties at the school— work alongside Miss Ruggles so his students won't miss out on their lessons. He suggested that perhaps Flora would tend to his recovery."

Mama nodded. "I'll do the teaching if Flora will do the nursing."

Dr. Bellows focused on Flora. "I know this isn't the kind of patient you're used to, but I'm asking as a favor to me. I'll stop by several times a day to check on him, help him to the outhouse, and such, if you'll stay bedside till Charlie's through the worst of this."

Grandma spoke up. "I'll help Flora."

Dr. Bellows rested a gentle hand on Grandma's rounded shoulder. "Thank you for your kind offer, but heed my words. You are not to be in the same room as Charlie. If you were to get what he's got, I'm not sure you'd recover. Flora has already had the flu. She's no longer susceptible."

Grandma shook a bent finger at him. "I tended Flora and never got sick."

"So you did, but there's no sense taking a foolish risk." Dr. Bellows shifted to Flora. "Can I count on you to help me see Charlie through his recovery?"

"Of course." Flora prayed she would be half as good at nursing Mr. Mason as Grandma had been to her.

"Good." Dr. Bellows turned to Papa and Toby. "If you fellows will each wrap a heavy scarf around your nose and mouth, I think you can help me get Charlie over here without too much danger of catching what he's got. Once we've settled him in the parlor, I want all but Flora to stay out of the sick room until his fever has broken. Now, I'd better get back to the hotel and get him ready for his move."

Papa nodded. "Toby and I will be there in a few minutes."

CHAPTER 34

Flora dashed up to her room to get dressed, then hurried down to the parlor. While Grandma kindled a fire in the parlor stove, Flora helped Mama make up a bed on the sofa and rearrange the furniture to accommodate a patient. No sooner had they finished their tasks than the men returned bearing a patient so pale and unshaven, Flora barely recognized him. He was so weak his legs seemed incapable of holding his own weight.

Dr. Bellows parked a brown leather bag near the table then helped Flora remove Charles's outer wraps and get him into bed. He shook with chills and coughed unproductively while asking in a voice barely above a whisper for more blankets and another pillow. Flora ran upstairs to strip the pillow and blankets from her own bed and with Dr. Bellows' help, tucked her pillow under Charles's head and snugged her blankets around his trembling body.

Dr. Bellows pulled a bottle of patent medicine from his leather bag and set it on the bedside stand. "Give him a teaspoon of this medicine about once every two hours when he's awake. He's due for another dose at five. But if he's sleeping, let him be. Sleep will do him more good than just about anything else. Trouble is he's too feverish to get much sleep right now."

A wave of sympathy welled up in Flora, remembering the feverish days and nights of her recent battle with the flu.

Dr. Bellows continued. "When he feels so feverish he starts throwing off the blankets, wipe him down with a cool, damp cloth. He'll probably need a change of night-shirt from time to time. I've put an extra one in his bag, along with a stack of handkerchiefs and some other things. Keep a pitcher of water and a cup nearby and try to get him to drink when he's awake. And feed him chicken broth if he'll take it. Now, I'd better get home and see how my other patients are doing. I'll be back in a couple of hours."

Flora followed him to the hallway, intending to see him out, but Dr. Bellows put his palm out. "I'll see my-self to the door, and if it's all right with you, I'll let myself in when I return. I'd hate to disturb Charlie with the doorknocker if he's asleep."

"I'll see you later, then." Flora returned to her patient, pulling up the most comfortable chair in the room to sit bedside.

Charles mumbled and sighed, and she quietly asked him if she could get him something, but he made no comprehensible reply. Evidently he was speaking out of the delirium of his fever.

Flora left the parlor only long enough to fetch a tea-spoon, a pitcher of drinking water, a tin cup, a wash basin of cold water, a towel, a washcloth, and a thunder jug. Then she positioned a footstool in front of her chair, doused the wall sconces, turned down the oil lamp on the bedside table, and sat down. Leaning back, she propped up her feet and closed her eyes. Visions of the red sleigh sprang to mind drawing her mouth into a smile. For a blissful moment she was in the cutter with Sven, gliding at a fast clip over the snowy road, cold wind whipping at her scarf while the heavy bear robe kept her warm.

Then Charles moaned and called a name that vaguely sounded like "Mother."

"It's Flora McAdams, Mr. Mason. Can I get you some water?" She poured a small amount into the cup, propped him up, and pressed the tin against his parched lips. They opened a little and she tipped the cup enough for him to drink, but it dribbled down his chin. She dried him off and leaned him back, pulling the covers snug around his shoulders and under his chin, praying for his recovery as she took to her chair again.

Pet and Big Boy padded into the room and nudged her for affection. She hugged them and told them to lie down. They settled on either side of her chair and she leaned back again, weary but unable to fall asleep for the tossing and turning of Charles and his mumbled words that she could not comprehend.

She rested in a state of semi-sleep until the morning whistle blew at five o'clock. Remembering Dr. Bellows' instructions about the medicine, she turned up the lamp to pour out a teaspoonful only to discover that despite the noise of the whistle, her patient was asleep.

With a prayer of thankfulness, she settled in her chair to catch a nap herself, waking an hour later to the sounds of Pet and Big Boy barking at the return of Dr. Bellows.

At the calming words of the good doctor, the dogs allowed him into the parlor. He went straight to his patient to check the temperature of Charles's forehead.

"He's even warmer than he was two hours ago. I'd like to sponge him down with cold water. Will you please step out of the room?"

She retreated to the hallway and closed the parlor door behind her. Head bowed, she petitioned the Lord for healing of the afflicted in Fayette. Her prayer ended when Dr. Bellows opened the door again.

Handing her the wash basin, he asked, "Would you be so good as to fill this with clean snow? I'm going to add a little cold water to it for sponging Charlie down. The ice-cold temperature will do him good."

She hastened to do his bidding, waiting in the hallway until the sponge bath had been completed and a clean, dry nightshirt had been put on Charles.

When she entered the parlor, she saw that he had been propped into a sitting position. He gazed up at her, blinking in an apparent struggle to focus.

"Miss McAdams? What are you doing here?" His voice barely broke a whisper.

Dr. Bellows spoke reassuringly. "She's taking care of you. You're in the McAdams' parlor. We moved you here last night. Remember?"

Charles shook his head with the sparest of movements.

"We're going to get you back on your feet again," said Flora, "but you need to take your medicine."

With an explanation to Dr. Bellows that Charles had slept through his five o'clock dose, she poured out a teaspoonful and carefully inserted it between her patient's narrowly parted lips.

Dr. Bellows offered Charles some water. He took a few sips then leaned back. Dr. Bellows set the empty cup on the table, lowered his patient to a prone position, and stood to go.

"I'll be back in another couple of hours."

CHAPTER 35

When the evening whistle blew, Flora paused in her sewing to inspect her work. She had finished setting in the second sleeve of a work shirt for her brother, and thankfully, her stitches looked even and the seam didn't pucker. The shirt would be a good Christmas gift for Toby, but she was sure it would also fit Sven. She pushed that thought from her head, reminding herself that wearing apparel was too personal to give him at Christmastime. But what *would* she give him?

With a sigh, she laid her sewing in her lap and picked up the piece of tablet paper lying on the bedside table and read again the note Lillian Ruggles had sent with Mama.

Charles,
My thoughts and prayers are with you, as are those of all the students, for a swift recovery. We miss you terribly! As ever, your devoted friend, Lillian.

Even though Flora had read it to him during one of his waking moments, she got the impression that in his condition, he wouldn't remember. Then the unwelcome thought passed through her mind that this difficult and wearisome day was only one of many long days to come. Despite the thoughts and prayers of Lillian and the students, Charles's recovery would not be swift.

Even so, blessings had emerged throughout the day. During a quiet spell in the morning, she had counted the money from raffle tickets. When Papa returned to work after the midday meal, Flora handed him a bag of coins amounting to $18 to be put in the safe at the Company Office. Eighteen dollars! She still could not believe such a large amount had been collected, and Christmas Eve was still three-and-a-half weeks away.

Flora was thankful, too, that when Dr. Bellows returned at mid-morning, he sent her out for a short but much-needed walk with Pet and Big Boy. And during the doctor's afternoon visit, she had spent some time working with the two difficult dogs she had rescued from Brinks. Responding to food rewards, they had begun learning to accept being leashed before being allowed out of their kennels. Well she knew that much more training was needed before they would allow anyone else to come near, but she thanked God for the small start on their path to better behavior.

Her thoughts of thankfulness were interrupted by the sound of the front door opening and the voices of Papa and Toby in lighthearted laughter over some comment that included the word "tickets". Pet and Big Boy abandoned their places by her chair and raced to the front hall. Flora leaned forward to place the back of her hand against her sleeping patient's forehead, then rose to stretch her legs and greet Papa and Toby.

Papa hung his jacket on the hall tree and put his arm around her waist, offering a hug and a shoulder to lean on. "How's Nurse McAdams?"

"Tired," she replied with a sigh.

"And your patient?"

"Still burning with fever."

Toby shrugged his jacket from his thick shoulders and turned to her. "Some of the biggest and strongest men on our shift were out sick today. Sure makes it rough on the rest of us."

Papa released Flora and reached into his pocket producing a folded piece of paper and a wide grin. "Here's something that ought to put a smile on your face."

Flora opened the slip to read a receipt for her $18 on deposit in the Company Safe. She smiled broadly and shoved the paper into her pocket. "Thanks, Papa."

Toby tossed his blue tweed cap onto a hook. "You should have heard the talk going around at work. When the fellows weren't grousing about the extra load put on them from so many being out sick, they argued about who was going to win the sleigh, bragging about how many tickets they were planning to buy before Christmas Eve. A couple of them almost got into a fight over it."

From the parlor came a mumbled request from Charles for water. Flora hastened to do her patient's bidding. When he had sipped a few swallows, she encouraged him to try some chicken broth, but by the time she had fetched a warm cup of it from the kitchen, he had fallen asleep. She sat again to take up her sewing, then set it aside to eat supper from the tray Grandma fixed and delivered to the parlor door. On it was a piece of the cake she had brought home from the hotel. The remembrance of the meal she had eaten there and the cake with the sleigh made her smile. For a moment she was no longer in the sick room, but across the table from Sven, her hands in his as he professed his feelings for her. How she yearned to be with him.

She picked up her fork and popped a piece of Grandma's creamed dried beef on biscuit into her mouth. Eyes closed, she tried to recall the flavor of the prime rib, pink and juicy, that Jane had served last night, but it was no use. She ate quickly, eager to get to dessert. Then she savored each bite slowly, letting the creamy red frosting melt on her tongue. She left nary a crumb of the chocolate cake on her plate.

No sooner had she returned her tray to the kitchen than Dr. Bellows arrived. Feeling the heat of Charles's forehead, he administered another cooling sponge bath, then headed out to check on Mr. Follo, who had taken ill with a high fever a few hours ago. The doctor had been gone but a few minutes when the sound of the doorknocker sent Pet and Big Boy into a fit of barking as they rushed to the front of the house. Flora opened the door a crack to see who was there, and finding Sven, she grabbed her cloak from the hall tree and slipped past the dogs to step outside.

The light from his lantern flickered softly against the sturdy lines of his cheek—the cheek Flora had kissed last night and yearned to kiss again when the time was right.

Her hand went unbidden to her own cheek as she recalled the kiss Sven had given her before his departure. Though the memory was vivid, the hours since had seemed like days. And the reason for their apparent endlessness jolted her back to the present.

"I can't walk the dogs tonight. Mr. Mason—"

"I heard. I came to give you something. Hold out your hands."

Coins jingled as he reached into his pocket. A smile tipped his mouth as he let several dimes cascade into her palms.

"Twenty tickets sold today!" He grinned.

Flora gasped. "Do you know what that means? With the money from last night, we already have $20! Thank you, thank you!" She dropped the coins into her own pocket, rose up on her toes, and planted a kiss on his cheek.

~~~

Warmth invaded Sven's cheeks and it had nothing to do with the fever that had knocked his boss off his feet. How he longed to stay with Flora, but work called. "I must go back to work. Mr. Follo—"

"I heard. Will you stop by again tomorrow?"

With a nod and an ocean of regret over the circumstances that prevented him from spending the evening with Flora, he turned to go, awash in the waves of longing that followed behind.

CHAPTER 36

One week later
Monday, December 8

The midday meal over, Flora leaned back in the chair where she had been rooted day and night for the past week. On the sofa beside her, a gaunt, stubble-faced Charles Mason continued to do battle with the persistent fever that had sapped his strength until he could not stand up without considerable support from Dr. Bellows. Weary to the bone, Flora closed her eyes and instantly drifted into a light sleep beset by the nightmarish routines of the past week. Administering of distasteful medicine, water taken in small sips through a pair of parched lips, chicken broth fed a spoonful at a time. Worst of all was the cough that came in fits day and night, racking Charles from head to toe and preventing both of them from getting more than a few minutes of sleep at a stretch.

She tried to ignore the new round of coughing but it sounded different, looser. He eyes opening a tiny bit, she

glanced in Charles's direction. He blew into a handkerchief, sighed, and shifted his position. Then he spoke
with a clarity she had not heard since his illness.

"Miss McAdams? I think the fever has broken."

Flora's eyes opened wide. She pressed the palm of her
right hand to his forehead. It did indeed seem normal.
Just to be sure, she checked again with her left hand.
"The Lord be praised, I think you're right! Can I get you
anything?"

He shook his head, then said, "On second thought,
you can get rid of this cough for me." He barely got the
words out before lapsing into another spasm of coughing. It was helping to clear his lungs of the infection, she
was certain, and she silently thanked God that her patient
was finally on the mend. A few minutes later he drifted
off to sleep, allowing Flora to do the same. As usual, the
nap was brief, interrupted this time not by coughing, but
by the arrival of Dr. Bellows who confirmed that his patient's temperature had returned to normal.

"You may have visitors, but keep it short. And don't
get any ideas about going back to teaching for another
couple of weeks. If you do too much too soon, you'll
have a relapse and be right back where you started."

"Yes, sir."

Dr. Bellows turned to Flora and stroked his beard
thoughtfully. "You look like you could use a week's
worth of sleep. Why don't you go on up to your own bed
and take a nap. Let your grandmother sit with Charles for
a while. The danger of him passing the flu to others is
over. I'll stop by tomorrow afternoon."

Flora offered a tired smile. "Thanks, Dr. Bellows. See you then."

He started for the door, then turned back, set down his bag, and hastily opened it. "I almost forgot to give you this." He removed a large brown medicine bottle that jingled. "The other day I got a stack of raffle tickets from Sven to sell. They went in a hurry."

She took the bottle full of coins in hand. "Thanks, Dr. Bellows!"

~~~

Eleven days later
Friday afternoon, December 19

Flora tidied up the parlor, folding the sheets and blankets that had been on the sofa while Charles, freshly bathed and shaved and fully dressed, sat in a chair by the front window, reading. Pet and Big Boy lay at his feet. By the time she had finished, Charles had leaned his head back and fallen asleep. She silently thanked God that he had improved considerably in the past week-and-a-half, but well she understood that he was far from recovering the strength he'd had before he'd taken sick. A diet of arrowroot and hot milk, coffee and eggs, milk toast, crackers and cream, and poached eggs had nurtured him for a week until he had regained an appetite for regular food, but the portions he ate were half that of a healthy man his size. Consequently, even a trip to the outhouse left him spent, and the possibility of his moving back to the hotel, where he would have to go down, then up a flight of stairs for each meal was still a few days off. With much rest, he would be strong enough to take the steamer to Escanaba to spend Christmas with his folks.

Flora stacked the pillows on top of the blankets and sheets and headed upstairs to store them in her room until bedtime. She set them on her sister's old bed, then, paused by her own bed and gazed at the troll Sven had given her. With a smile, she sat down to daydream of the man who had stolen her heart.

Though Sven's quiet ways often left Flora wondering about his unspoken thoughts, she thanked God that he had come by every evening since their dinner at the hotel to bring her news of tickets sold. And after Charles's fever had broken, Sven had resumed his habit of helping her walk her dogs. Only now, they had added the boxers to their outings. What a sight they made, Sven with Pet and Big Boy, and she with the two boxers. Although Rocky and Jack still needed constant reminders to heel while on leash, they would soon be ready for a new home, if she could find someone to take them.

She pushed that thought to the back of her mind and put her troll away to focus again on the task at hand—preparing the parlor for the friends who had been invited to join her, Charles, and Toby for the evening. Sven, Lillian, and Elin, along with Joseph Marew and Maggie Coughlin, would all be coming at half-past seven, and with Christmas less than a week away, Flora had much to do to make the parlor look festive and to help Grandma prepare the wassail and cookies.

CHAPTER 37

When the laughter had died down, and Charles's humorous conclusion to the "Endless Story" that had been composed by the guests had taken far longer than the one minute allowed, Flora held out the basket of "forfeits" to him. On folded papers were the silly penalties that Charles had thought up and written out while she had decorated the parlor with pine boughs and red ribbons.

"Pick one," Flora demanded.

"Must I?" he asked with a heavy sigh. "Look, I already have two others. And me, so weak and frail from illness that my legs can barely carry my own weight."

Sven clucked his tongue in mock sympathy. "Poor fellow."

"You don't need good legs to pick a forfeit," Toby said.

"Or to carry one out," said Joseph.

"Maybe we've tired him so, he no longer has the strength to reach into the basket." Lillian's eyes sparkled.

"I think he is stalling because he is the one who made up the forfeits," said Elin.

Charles shook his head. "Not true, not true!" He reached for the basket, his hand resting against Flora's while he fumbled with the slips of paper.

Flora thought nothing of the contact. She set the forfeits aside. "The next game is 'If you love me dearest, smile!'" She turned to Sven. "You're 'it'!" To the others, she said, "Remember, if you smile when you say 'I love you dearest, but I just can't smile,' you're 'it'!"

Sven stood in the center of the room, glanced at each of the young ladies present, then approached Elin, speaking to her in a monotone. "If you love me dearest, smile."

Elin replied solemnly, "I love you dearest, but I just can't smile."

Sven turned and approached Maggie, demanding in a low, gruff voice, "If you love me dearest, smile."

Without a hint of a smile, she replied in a low, surly voice, "I love you dearest, but I just can't smile."

Joseph, Charles, and Toby began to chuckle, infecting the ladies with laughter.

Sven smiled, then pulled an exaggerated frown and turned to Lillian. "If you love me dearest, smile."

Lillian covered her mouth with her hand, wiping away the smile on her lips. Then she replied with neither smile nor feeling, "I love you dearest, but I just can't smile." Sven turned to Flora. He winked, blinked, twitched his eyebrows and nose, and twisted his lips into the most lopsided position she had ever seen, then asked in a high, squeaky voice, "If you love me dearest, smile."

Flora lapsed into giggles. Unable to talk, she stood to take her turn as "it". Still chuckling, she approached Charles and said, "If you love me dearest, smile."

He turned deadpan, his voice quiet. "I love you dearest . . ." He paused to struggle against a smile.

In a moment of childish silliness inspired by Sven's earlier performance, Flora stuck her thumbs in her ears and waved her fingers at Charles.

He burst into laughter, as did Flora and most of the others.

She pointed to Charles. "You're 'it'!" But when she sat down next to Sven, she noticed that he wasn't laughing. During games of Adverbs, Ten Fine Birds, Botticelli, and Riddles, Flora took great satisfaction in watching her friends enjoying themselves. It was obvious that Lillian was hopelessly in love with Charles, Toby and Elin were quietly devoted to each other, and Maggie and Joseph never missed an opportunity to tease one another—a sure sign of their mutual affection. But Sven seemed too quiet.

When the last riddle had been solved, Flora stood. "It's time for forfeits. I'll begin." She opened one of her forfeits and read, "'Kiss your own shadow.'" Turning the lamps very low, she lit a candle and approached Sven. Holding it so as to cast her shadow against his cheek, she kissed him, thankful when a smile returned to his face. But it vanished too quickly, and made only rare appearances while the others performed their forfeits. It seemed to her that everyone but Sven was in jolly good humor.

When she served the wassail and cookies, conversation frequently elicited laughter from all but Sven. Was he coming down with the flu and feeling out of sorts?

Guests took their leave at ten o'clock so as to preserve Charles's strength and allow the working men to get a good night's sleep. When only Charles and Sven remained, she pulled on her cloak to see Sven out, desirous of a little privacy to inquire of his health and say good night. They stepped out onto the front stoop and she pressed her hand to his forehead.

"Are you feeling well? You seemed too quiet. I thought maybe you were coming down with the flu, but you don't seem to have a fever."

Sven shook his head. "No fever."

In the dim light spilling from the parlor window, she studied the pensive look he gave her. And though it was too dark to tell, she was fairly certain his changeable eyes were gray rather than blue. "You've been awfully quiet tonight— too quiet. Is something bothering you?"

"No . . . yes . . . . Mason is sweet on you!"

"Charles?" She shook her head vigorously. "Lillian is head over heels for him. She's visited him every day after school since his fever lifted. And he seems sufficiently appreciative of her, too."

Sven appeared unconvinced. "When will he move back to hotel?"

Flora shrugged. "After the first of the year, I suppose. He's planning to visit his folks in Escanaba for Christmas and New Year's, then go back to teaching when school resumes."

Sven remained stone-faced and silent.

Flora continued. "He really isn't strong enough to live at the hotel right now, taking those stairs three times a day for meals. Besides, there are only a few days left—"

"Flora, will you marry me?"

Had she heard correctly? Had he asked...? No, couldn't be. She rushed on. "If you saw how much time Charles spends napping in a day, you'd know—"

Sven pressed his finger to her lips, and gazed intensely into her eyes. "Flora, please tell. Will you marry me?"

Her heart stopped, then raced. She struggled for words. "Did you . . . did you ask me to *marry* you?"

Sven nodded and smiled.

She drew a sharp breath. Her words tumbled out. "Good glory! Yes! I will marry you!" She planted a kiss on his cheek, then threw her arms about his neck and squeezed hard.

His arms wrapped tightly about her and pulled her against the length of him. Moments later he released her, and taking her face in his hands, his lips descended to hers, covering them in a soft, lingering kiss that sent her heart soaring to the stars. When the kiss ended, he took her by the shoulders, his gaze locked on hers.

"Go inside and tell Mason you and I will be married."

"When?"

"Now! Go!" He turned her toward the door.

She looked back over her shoulder. "That's not what I meant. When will we be married?"

"As soon as I find a place for us to live. Now go. Tell Mason." He reached for the doorknob.

She turned to him once more, giving him a kiss on the cheek. When she stepped inside, her feet barely touched the ground.

~~~

Five days later
Wednesday, December 24

Awakened by the five o'clock whistle, Flora could hardly believe the day of the raffle drawing had arrived. The last five days had taken on an additional pair of wings, it seemed, sending one day soaring into the next on a blissful cloud of Christmas and wedding plans. Besides wanting to spend every available minute with Sven, Flora needed to finish hemming the handkerchiefs she would give him for Christmas.

She smiled at the thought of the Christmas gift Sven had given her early. Out of season, he had somehow managed to find her a brand new straw hat with a brim untouched by cat's teeth. A thrill went through her at the thought that, by the time the weather turned warm enough to wear it she would already be married with a home and animal shelter of her own.

Turning her thoughts to the day ahead, she remembered that she and Grandma had promised to bake the gingerbread men and women that would be given to the sixty students at the Christmas program tonight. She sprang from her bed to start her day. An hour later, she was pressing raisin buttons into the cutouts on the cookie sheet while Grandma rolled out another batch of dough, talking as she worked.

"That young man of yours is just full of surprises. Who would have thought that he could be so quick to find a place for you to live, and that the two of you would be getting married three days after Christmas?"

Flora chuckled. "And who would have thought that Sven could sell over five hundred raffle tickets on the sleigh? I still can't believe that we have put over $50 into the Company safe from ticket sales. Think how far it will go to build shelters and buy supplies for the hurting and homeless cats and dogs in this town."

Grandma offered a wry smile. "I fear that the welfare of this town's pets has had little bearing on folks' determination to spend extravagantly on chances to win that sleigh. I never thought a conveyance could be *too* beautiful, but that sleigh is. It has turned otherwise intelligent and frugal folks into a greedy, covetous lot of spendthrifts."

Grandma's words assaulted Flora's heart with a dozen pinpricks. "Good glory, it's not Sven's fault that the sleigh came out so well, or that folks want to own it. Yes, Sven did work long and hard on the sleigh, but he had plenty of help."

"Too much help, maybe." Grandma raised an arthritic finger. "Don't get me wrong. I'm happy for Sven's and your success, but it seems that everyone who had a hand in fixing up that old cutter feels especially entitled to own it."

"And tonight will tell who the winner is," Flora replied cheerfully as she pulled a tray of freshly baked gingerbread people out of the oven and slid in the ones she had just decorated.

CHAPTER 38

"Happy Christmas to all, and to all a good-night!" little Annie exclaimed, bringing the Christmas program to a conclusion. She curtsied to a hearty round of applause and stepped off the podium to join her family in the front row.

When the applause had died down, Mama stepped onto the podium. She presented the perfect image of a teacher with her dark, silver-streaked hair center-parted and pulled into a bun at the back of her neck. Her charcoal gray wool dress had a closely fitted bodice and a draped skirt, the perfect combination of stylishness and practicality.

A smile brightened Mama's face as she gazed out at the audience. "I have a gift for each of the children. Then, my daughter, Flora, will draw the winner of the sleigh."

While Flora helped Mama, Grandma, and Lillian pass out one large gingerbread cookie to each of the sixty children, Sven carried in the keg containing the raffle tickets and placed it on the teacher's desk.

The room, already packed with folks standing along the walls, became even more jammed as others who had no kin in the Christmas program wedged their way inside for the raffle drawing.

Flora stepped behind the teacher's desk and surveyed the audience, recognizing the faces of many who had bought tickets on the sleigh, others who had contributed substantially to the labor and materials needed for its restoration, and some who had done both. Dr. and Mrs. Bellows sat in the back row beside Joe Harris and his wife Harriet, and Superintendent J.B. Kitchen and his wife Alison.

Behind them stood Papa, Toby, and Elin. To Flora's right were Joseph Marew and Maggie Coughlin, Mr. Hines from the sawmill, Mr. Ferris from the stock barn, Mr. Grennell from the Carpenter Shop, and Mr. Powell from the Company Store. To the left were Thomas Young from the furnace, Mr. Cumberland from the Blacksmith Shop, George and Clara Harris, Henry Pinchin and his folks, and Charles. Along with those she recognized were dozens whose names she did not know but whose faces she had seen when selling taffy tarts. Congenial conversation came to an end and expressions rich with expectation subtly shifted to impatience.

Someone said, "Get on with it!"

Others chimed in.

"Yeah! Get on with it!"

"Pick the winner!"

"Draw a ticket!"

"Pick *mine.*"

"No, *mine!*"

"I bought more tickets than you did! She's gonna pick *mine!*"

Flora raised her hands, palms out. "Quiet, everybody, please." She reached for the handle on the keg and began cranking it to mix up the tickets. "I want to thank you all for your interest in winning the sleigh. You have contributed substantially toward the care and feeding of the hurting and homeless creatures of Fayette." She cranked the keg around three more times, then opened the padlock and reached inside. Stirring the tickets with her hand, she grabbed hold of one and pulled it out.

The room grew silent.

Her hand trembled with excitement, but she had no trouble reading the name that had been scrawled there in bold strokes. With a huge smile, she gazed out at the audience. "The winner of the sleigh is Dr. Bellows!"

A couple of people applauded. Joe Harris slapped his friend on the back and congratulated him.

Someone said, "That's not fair!"

Another said, "It was fixed!"

Still another said, "She picked her friend!"

And yet another claimed, "She palmed Bellows' ticket! I saw her!"

Flora's heart raced. "Good glory, I did no such thing!"

Arguments broke out.

Sven, Toby, Papa, Mama, and Grandma boldly defended her.

Some believed them.

Others claimed fraud.

Men rose to their feet, shouting in each other's faces. Flora laid the ticket on the desk and turned to Sven.

He put his arm tightly about her and practically lifted her off her feet, carrying her toward the door to the cloakroom. Papa, Mama, Toby, and Grandma followed.

Mr. Hines grabbed Sven by the shoulder. "Was it fixed, Jorgensen?"

He shook his head vigorously. "Of course not!" Pressing forward, they encountered George Harris. "I'm disappointed in you, Flora! I thought we all had a fair chance at this! "

"You did!" Flora claimed.

Thomas Young said, "I don't believe you!"

Maggie Coughlin stepped in front of Flora. "Nor do I! I never should have lifted a finger to upholster that sleigh!"

Joseph Marew shook his finger at Flora. "And I never should have lifted a paintbrush to it!"

Sven pushed past them, taking Flora with him. They were two feet from the door when Mr. Grennell grabbed Sven by the arm.

"You're not getting off so easy, Jorgensen!"

Sven nudged Flora toward the cloakroom. "Go home before you get hurt."

Angry and resolute, she planted her feet. "I won't go until this is settled!"

Grennell said, "Doggoned right, you'll settle it! I want my money back!"

Mr. Cumberland pressed in. "So do I!"

Flora looked straight into Mr. Cumberland's eyes. "If you can find anything amiss about this drawing, I will gladly return your money."

Angry voices demanded refunds. Folks jostled, pushed, and shoved until Flora, Sven, and her kin were surrounded by irate ticket holders.

Again, Sven pleaded with her. "Go home! Now!"

"But—"

Papa cut her off. "If you have any respect at all for the man you're about to marry, you'll do as he says."

"Papa's right," said Toby. "Go home with Mama and Grandma. Leave this to us men."

Mama laid Flora's cloak on her shoulders, linked one arm with her and the other with Grandma, and edged through the crowd to the door.

From outside, they could hear angry voices growing louder.

~~~

Inside, Sven pressed his way to the front of the classroom, ignoring the barrage of accusations and demands for refunds hurled at him. Stepping onto the chair behind the teacher's desk, he raised his arms in an effort to quiet the mob, but they only grew louder.

Suddenly, a shrill whistle, loud as a train, rent the air.

The place fell silent.

Joe Harris's gravelly voice rang out from the back of the room.

"Let the man speak! And if he's cheated anyone, let him say so!"

CHAPTER 39

Sven's heart raced. His face burned. His arms crossed on his chest, he organized his thoughts in English, offering an economy of carefully chosen words. "I have cheated no one. Nor has Flora. Dr. Bellows bought the most tickets. He deserves to win. If you do not believe, then count them."

"Yes! Count them!" Dr. Bellows said.

"Count them!" echoed throughout the room until voices rose to a dull roar.

Joe Harris whistled again.

Again silence fell.

Superintendent Kitchen stood. "I'll appoint a committee to count the tickets and a committee to verify the count. Hines, Mason, Grennell, Cumberland. Count the tickets. Oliver Ferris, Joseph Marew, William Pinchin, Joe Harris, verify the count."

Sven dumped the tickets onto the desktop, set the keg aside, then stepped back. Head down, eyes closed, he silently prayed for truth to prevail and reason to reign. A hand came to rest on his shoulder. He opened his eyes to find Mr. McAdams.

He spoke quietly. "It will be over soon, son, and all will see that nothing was amiss."

Sven nodded, yet silently worried whether hard feelings could be mended. His apprehension increased when he heard someone murmur, "This isn't right," followed by much whispering and passing about of tickets evidently in question.

A minute or two later, when it appeared as though Charles Mason had brought the counters to a consensus, he picked up a piece of chalk and began marking names and numbers on the blackboard.

Dr. Bellows—20	Hines—6
J.B. Kitchen—15	Cumberland—6
Mrs. Bellows—10	Ferris—6
J. Harris—10	Grennell—6
S. Kitchen—10	T. Young—6
W. Pinchin—8	C. Mason—5
H. Pinchin—7	A. Powell—5
Marew—7	M. Coughlin—4
G. Harris—6	J. Meehan—4

All others—less than 4 ea.

Now the counters stepped back to allow the verifiers to do their work. Sven was certain that mistakes had been made and would be corrected.

Checking one stack of sorted tickets at a time and comparing it with the number on the board, the verifying committee checked each name off until all were checked.

Superintendent Kitchen stood at the blackboard and read the results, pointing to names and numbers as he worked his way down the two columns. Even though Charles Mason's printing was perfectly legible and large enough to read from the back row, many of the laborers, especially the recent immigrants, could neither read nor write more than their own name.

Finished with his reading, the Superintendent said, "Does anyone disagree with this count? If so, speak up now!"

Mr. Ferris jumped to his feet. "You got my count wrong!"

"How many tickets did you buy?"

"Five!" Ferris replied firmly. "I bought five, but on the board, it says six!"

Maggie Coughlin rose to her feet. "My count is wrong, too. I bought *three* tickets, not four."

John Meehan said, "So did I. And you all know I never forget a fact."

Several others stood up, complaining of a count different than the number on the board until the discussion fell into confusion.

A loud whistle from Joe Harris restored order.

The Superintendent said, "Sit down, folks, *please*." When they were seated, he said, "Give me a show of hands. How many people bought *fewer* tickets than the number on the board?"

Sven counted ten hands in the air, each belonging to someone who had worked side by side with him restoring the sleigh.

The Superintendent continued. "Put your hands down. How many people bought *more* tickets than the number on the board?"

Not a hand went up.

Superintendent Kitchen turned to the counters and verifiers standing behind him. "Does anyone of you have an explanation for Mr. Ferris, Miss Coughlin, and the others who raised their hands?"

Charles Mason stepped forward. "Mr. Superintendent, sir, when we counted the tickets, Mr. Hines, Mr. Cumberland, and Mr. Grennell each counted one more in their name than they had bought, and each said that the handwriting on one of their tickets was not their own. They also noticed that the additional tickets seemed to have been written out by the same person, and that person had the same handwriting as on Dr. Bellows' tickets."

Superintendent Kitchen turned to Dr. Bellows. "How about it, Doc? Did you buy tickets and write other peoples' names on them?"

"I did," he quietly replied.

Mr. Ferris jumped up. "But why?"

"It was my own private gesture of appreciation for the time and labor that you folks put into the sleigh."

Superintendent Kitchen said, "So you bought forty tickets altogether. Twenty tickets were for yourself, ten tickets were for your wife, and you wrote other people's names on ten tickets. Is that right?"

Dr. Bellows nodded.

The Superintendent picked up an eraser and faced the crowd. "Then it's settled. Bellows wins the sleigh. I'm going to erase the blackboard, and while I do, I suggest you each erase doubt and disappointment from your minds and hearts, wish each other a Happy Christmas, and go home to enjoy the rest of this Christmas Eve with your families."

Mr. Ferris jumped up. "Superintendent, with your permission, may I say something?"

Kitchen began to shake his head.

Ferris persisted. "There's a whole lotta folks here that owe the good doctor an apology, and I sure hope you'll offer it to him before you leave. And there's a young lady by the name of Miss Flora McAdams who left here right after the drawing all upset. You folks never shoulda accused her of wrongdoing. She's done nothin' but help folks in this town with their cats and dogs, fixin' them up and never askin' a dime in return. Then when she come up with an idea to do it better by raisin' some money, what'd you do? Accuse her of cheatin'! You oughta be ashamed of yourselves! Ashamed enough to go to her now and apologize!"

CHAPTER 40

Flora paced the parlor, her emotions tied in knots by the twin demons, anger and fear; anger over unjust accusations from neighbors and friends, and fear for the safety of Sven, Papa, and Toby. Pet, Big Boy, and the boxers, Rocky and Jack, lay near the parlor stove.

Mama chased Pet and Big Boy out of the way to pull two chairs and a table close to the stove. Grandma set a tea tray on the table, then she and Mama sat down.

Flora turned to Mama and Grandma. "Ruined! My Christmas is ruined!"

Grandma said, "I surely wouldn't let a few unkind—and untrue—words ruin Christmas. Here, have some tea. It'll make you feel better."

Flora took the cup gratefully and sipped. "Thanks, Grandma. I do feel better. I think." Then anger and fear overtook her once again. She silently begged God to protect Sven and to bring about a peaceful resolution to the rancor at the schoolhouse.

She thought about the people and pets she had helped. A dagger sliced through her, recalling how Mr. Hines,

Thomas Young, Maggie Coughlin, and Mr. Grennell had turned against her. Their betrayal cut deep, and she wasn't sure the friendships would ever mend.

She finished her tea and Grandma refilled her cup. "Nothing like tea to lift your spirits."

Mama rose, went to the front parlor window, and pulled back the curtain. "I thought I heard voices."

Flora privately prayed that Sven was on his way to her. Before her prayer was even finished, she too heard voices, not talking but singing.

"I do believe some folks are coming up our street, caroling," said Mama.

"They must have come from the school," said Grandma. "'Twasn't another soul in town but for the laborers at the furnace when we came home."

A moment later, the singing sent the dogs into a ferocious round of barking and Flora rose to calm them. Her efforts were made unnecessary when Papa and Toby came through the door, grabbed all four dogs by their collars, and led them to the back room.

Sven stepped inside, followed by a large band of carolers who gathered around Flora filling the hallway, the parlor, and spilling into the dining room and kitchen.

Their joyful message enveloped Flora.

"We wish you a Merry Christmas, we wish you a Merry Christmas, we wish you a Merry Christmas and a Happy New Year! Good tidings we bring. . ."

While the carolers finished their verse, all those who had been quick to level accusations of unfairness at Flora—George Harris, Thomas Young, Maggie Coughlin, and Joseph Marew—now surrounded her in song. Be-

hind them were those who had been angry with Sven—
Mr. Hines, Mr. Grennell, and Mr. Cumberland. And with
them were other neighbors and friends whom she'd seen
at the school.

When the verse ended, George Harris spoke. "I'm
sorry for what I said to you at the schoolhouse, Flora. I
know now how wrong I was. Will you please accept my
apology?" He stuck out his hand.

"Of course, George." She placed her hand in his for a
hearty handshake.

Thomas Young approached Flora. "I'm sorry, too.
Real sorry. You done nothing but kindness for my cat
and me and I returned it with anger. Forgive me?"

She nodded and shook his hand. The pattern of apologies and handshakes repeated with Maggie Coughlin,
Joseph Marew, and many others who had been at the raffle and questioned its outcome.

The apologies over, Mr. Hines shouted, "Three cheers
for Miss Flora McAdams!"

In united voices, all shouted, "Hip, hip, hooray! Hip,
hip, hooray! Hip, hip, hooray!"

Then they launched into song. "For she's a jolly good
lady, for she's a jolly good lady. . ."

The cheerful voices put a smile on Flora's face and
gladness in her heart.

When the song ended, Mr. Hines called out, "Merry
Christmas, Miss McAdams!"

His words were echoed again and again as Flora's
visitors departed leaving only her family and Sven beside her in the hallway.

Papa put his hand on Flora's shoulder. "I could do with a good hot cup of tea and one of those gingerbread cookies, if there are any left."

"There's plenty of tea already brewed. I'll fetch it." Grandma headed for the kitchen.

"I'll fetch more cups and saucers." Mama followed Grandma.

Toby started after them. "I'll fill a plate with cookies."

Papa laughed. "And help yourself to an extra one in the process. Guess there's nothing left for me to do but settle into my favorite chair in the parlor and put my feet up."

When the others had gone, leaving Sven alone with Flora in the front hall, he drew her into his arms and gazed into her eyes.

Flora searched the blue-gray eyes fixed on hers, basking in the tenderness and affection that transcended words, and silently thanked God for putting such a marvelous man in her life. She was about to put her thoughts into words when Sven spoke, his voice barely above a whisper.

"This Christmas is my best ever, because of you. I love you, Flora. Merry Christmas!"

She had started to return the sentiment when his mouth covered hers, drinking in her words and sealing their love for many Christmases to come.

Taffy Tarts

(recipe from Carol Adriance, a friend of the author's mother)

1 cup brown sugar
Pinch of salt
1 egg
1 teaspoon vanilla
Butter size of walnut
(Beat well.)

(The above is the filling for an unbaked tart shell. No directions were given for the shell, baking temperature, or time.)

ABOUT DONNA WINTERS

Donna adopted Michigan as her home state in 1971 when she moved from a small town outside of Rochester, New York. She began penning novels in 1982 while working full time for an electronics company in Grand Rapids.

She resigned in 1984 following a contract offer for her first book. Since then, she has written several romance novels for various publishers, including Thomas Nelson Publishers, Zondervan Publishing House, Guideposts, and Bigwater Publishing LLC. Her nonfiction writing has been published by Chalfont House.

Her husband, Fred, a retired American History teacher, shares her enthusiasm for history. Together, they visit historical sites, restored villages, museums, and lake ports, purchasing books and reference materials and taking photos.

Donna lived her first sixty-five years in states bordering on the Great Lakes. During twelve of those years she lived next door to Fayette Historic State Park. Her familiarity and fascination with the Great Lakes and her longtime residence in the heart of Great Lakes Country provide the perfect background for writing *Great Lakes Romances*®.

MORE GREAT LAKES ROMANCES®

To read about more women of Fayette, visit

http://greatlakesromances.com/collection-titles/fayette-times

A Time to Love, **Eighth in the series of Great Lakes Romances®** (Set in Fayette, Michigan, 1868.) The new iron-smelting town of Fayette, Michigan held no promise for sixteen-year-old Lavinia McAdams. The moment she arrived, she took an instant disliking to its muddy streets, acrid smoke, and dirty furnace men. The sooner she could return to her hometown in Canada, the better. Then Huck Harrigan came along to challenge her thinking and soften her iron will. Could she really find happiness in this raw, new town with a "pig iron" Irishman from across the bay?

A Time to Laugh, **Ninth in the series of Great Lakes Romances®** (Set in Fayette, Michigan in 1879.) The greatest passion of Flora McAdams' life has always been her love of animals. From girlhood she had made it her mission to care for orphaned wild creatures and hurting family pets in the pig iron town of Fayette. Now, at age eighteen, she has no lack of four-footed patients needing her skill, and no time or thought of romance, until a quiet Norwegian machinist comes to town. Sven Jorgensen hoped his first encounter with the feisty Flora McAdams would be his last. Whether at the village vegetable garden or the town racetrack, he can't seem to avoid her. But time works miracles. And after witnessing her transformation of hurting, homeless canines into healthy, loving pets, his thoughts of her are altered as well. Can he somehow convince her that he has much more than friendship in mind for their future?

A Time to Leave, **Tenth in the series of Great Lakes Romances®** (Set in Fayette, Michigan, 1885-1891.) At age fourteen, Violet Harrigan encounters dual tragedies: the death of her father, and the resulting need to move several miles north to Fayette. The situation is more than she can bear. But a true friend sticks closer than a brother. Guy Legard visits Violet faithfully. Months turn into years, and the seed of friendship blossoms into love. Then Guy disappears into the woods for several long months and Violet turns her attention to a suave and debonair newcomer, Reggie Vanderveen. Will he steal her away to a new life of excitement in Boston, or can Guy rekindle the flame of enduring love?

Picturing Fayette (a photobook of Fayette Historic Townsite) Fayette Historic Townsite in the Upper Peninsula of Michigan offers visitors a step back in time to a nineteenth century company town. Here, nestled beneath a towering limestone bluff on Lake Michigan, the Jackson Iron Company operated two iron smelting furnaces. From December 25, 1867 to December 1, 1890, hot iron poured forth into casting houses, was cooled and separated into "pigs", and shipped to Ohio aboard schooners. Today, several original structures give testimony to Michigan's industrial past—from the laborers' log cabin, to the managers' salt box homes, to the "Big White House" on the hill that was occupied by the superintendent. In the center of all these stands the working core of the once-thriving village—the furnace stacks, casting houses, company store, warehouse, town hall, company office, machine shop, and hotel. Through the pages of this book, tour this fascinating open air museum that offers million-dollar views of the harbor, bay, and quaint remnants from nearly 150 years ago. Quotes from newspapers of that era serve as captions, bringing the town to life. Fayette Historic Townsite is without a doubt one of the best-preserved company towns in America and a gem of Michigan history that is unlike any other.

http://greatlakesromances.com/collection-titles/fayette-times

www.ingramcontent.com/pod-product-compliance
Lightning Source LLC
Chambersburg PA
CBHW061945170626
46813CB00006B/2536